PRIDE OF EAGLES

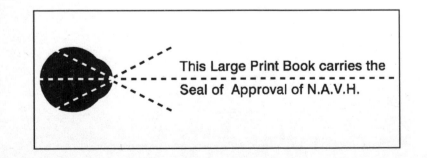

This Large Print Book carries the
Seal of Approval of N.A.V.H.

PRIDE OF EAGLES

WILLIAM W. JOHNSTONE WITH J. A. JOHNSTONE

WHEELER PUBLISHING

A part of Gale, Cengage Learning

GALE
CENGAGE Learning™

Detroit • New York • San Francisco • New Haven, Conn • Waterville, Maine • London

GALE
CENGAGE Learning-

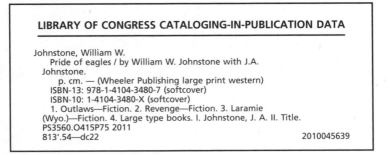

LIBRARY OF CONGRESS CATALOGING-IN-PUBLICATION DATA

Johnstone, William W.
    Pride of eagles / by William W. Johnstone with J.A. Johnstone.
        p. cm. — (Wheeler Publishing large print western)
    ISBN-13: 978-1-4104-3480-7 (softcover)
    ISBN-10: 1-4104-3480-X (softcover)
    1. Outlaws—Fiction. 2. Revenge—Fiction. 3. Laramie (Wyo.)—Fiction. 4. Large type books. I. Johnstone, J. A. II. Title.
    PS3560.O415P75 2011
    813'.54—dc22   2010045639

Published in 2011 by arrangement with Pinnacle Books, an imprint of Kensington Publishing Corp.

Printed in the United States of America
1 2 3 4 5 6 7 15 14 13 12 11

PRIDE OF EAGLES

ONE

Distorted by shimmering heat waves, the town of Picacho, Arizona Territory, lay baking in the sun as Falcon rode into town. To the side of one of the houses, a woman was washing clothes while two children played on the ground beside her. A dog walked up for a closer examination of Falcon, but it was too hot for him to offer any challenge, so he turned and withdrew to the shade of the building.

Picacho was built along the Southern Pacific Railroad, the steel ribbons that gave it life. In fact, it was the railroad that brought Falcon to Picacho. He was coming back from his silver mine, located in the Cabibi Mountains, near Oro Blanco. He had bought the mine from Doc Holliday, but his friend had neglected to tell him that, in order to make the mine productive, he would have to deal with some hostile Apache Indians.

7

He took care of that, and was now on his way back to his home in MacCallister Valley, Colorado. He was in Picacho because it was the nearest place he could catch a train.

The largest structure in town had a big picture of a golden mug of beer painted on the false front of the building. Alongside the mug of beer, in large red letters, outlined in black, was the name of the saloon: THE BROWN DIRT COWBOY.

Dismounting in front of the saloon, Falcon tied his horse off at the hitching rail, then stepped up on the porch to go inside. If anyone happened to be looking in this direction at that point in time, they would have seen a big man, standing a little over six feet tall. His shoulders were wide and muscular and his waist was flat. Pale blue eyes stared out from a chiseled face. He had wheat-colored hair, which he wore short and neat. He was wearing a long-sleeved red shirt, a buckskin vest, and Levi's jeans, which were tucked into long black boots.

Falcon had been thinking about a cold beer for the last two days, and he could almost taste it now as he pushed his way through the batwing doors.

Hanging gourds of evaporating water made the interior of the saloon at least ten degrees cooler than it was outside. It was dark in the saloon, so dark that Falcon had to stand for a moment until his eyes adjusted to the lack of light.

He took out a long, thin cheroot and lit it by striking a match on the handle of his Colt .44. He took a few puffs, then squinting his eyes through the cloud of smoke, surveyed the saloon he had just entered. The bar was made of unfinished, wide-plank boards, with an attached ledge at the bottom to be used as a foot rail. There was no mirror behind the bar, but there was a shelf with an assortment of liquor bottles. A bartender with pomade-slick hair and a waxed mustache was standing behind the bar with his arms folded across his chest.

Over the last few years Falcon could almost define his life by places like this: fly-blown towns, crude saloons, and green whiskey. Although he could easily afford the high life, Falcon had been wandering around ever since his wife, Marie Gentle Breeze, herself an Indian, had been killed by Indians. Sometimes the cold sweats and killing rages still plagued him, but for the most part now, he was able to put that behind him.

Falcon stepped up to the bar.

"What can I do you for?" the bartender asked.

"Is your beer cold?"

"Colder than a mountain stream," he answered.

"All right, I'll take a glass," Falcon said.

The bartender drew the beer and put it front of Falcon. "Just passing through, are you?" the bartender asked.

"Yes," Falcon replied without elaborating. He picked up the mug and took a long drink before he turned to look around the place. Although it was mid-afternoon, the saloon was nearly full, the customers drawn by the fact that this was the coolest building in town.

As he stood at the bar, a tall, broad-shouldered, bearded man stepped in through the back door. At first Falcon wondered why he had come through the back door; then he saw that a star was barely showing from beneath the vest he was wearing. The sheriff pointed a gun toward one of the tables.

"I just got a telegram about you, Kofax," the lawman said. "You should'a had better sense than to come back to a town where ever'one knows you."

"Let it be, Calhoun," Kofax replied. "I ain't staying here long. I'm just waitin' around for the train to take me out of here."

The sheriff shook his head. "I don't think

10

so. You won't be catchin' the train today," he said. "You're goin' to jail."

Kofax stood up slowly, and stepped away from the table.

"Well, now, you're plannin' on takin' me there all by yourself, are you, Calhoun?" Kofax asked.

The quiet calm of the barroom grew tense, and most of the other patrons in the bar stood up and moved to both sides of the room, giving the sheriff and Kofax a lot of room.

Only Falcon didn't move. He stayed by the bar, sipping his beer and watching the drama play out before him.

"You can make this a lot easier by dropping your gun belt," the sheriff said.

Kofax chuckled, but there was no humor in his laugh. "Well, now, you see, there you go. I don't plan to make it easy for you," he said.

"Shuck out of that gun belt like I told you, slow and easy," the sheriff ordered.

Falcon saw something then that the sheriff either didn't see, or didn't notice. Kofax's eyes flicked upward for an instant, then back down toward the sheriff. Kofax smiled, almost confidently, at the sheriff.

"Sorry, Calhoun, but like I said, I don't plan to make this easy for you."

Curious as to why Kofax wasn't more nervous, Falcon glanced up and saw a man standing at the top of the stairs. The man was aiming a pistol at the sheriff's back. That was what Kofax had seen when he cut his eyes upward, and that was what was giving him such supreme confidence.

"Sheriff, look out!" Falcon shouted.

"Stay out of this, you son of a bitch!" the man at the top of the stairs shouted. He turned his pistol toward Falcon.

Falcon dropped his beer and pulled his own pistol, firing just as the man at the top of the stairs fired. The shooter's bullet missed Falcon and hit a whiskey bottle that was sitting on the bar. The impact sent a shower of whiskey and splinters of glass.

Falcon's shot caught the shooter in the chest, and he dropped his pistol and clasped his hand over the entry wound, then looked down at himself as blood began to spill between his fingers. The shooter's eyes rolled up in his head and he tumbled forward, sliding down the stairs, following his clattering pistol all the way down. He lay motionless at the bottom, his head and shoulders on the floor, his legs still on the steps.

Although the sound of the two gunshots had riveted everyone's attention, the situation between Kofax and the sheriff continued to play out, and almost before the sound of the first two gunshots had faded, two more shots rang out. The sheriff's bullet struck Kofax in the neck, forcing him back against the cold, wood-burning stove, causing him to hit it with such impact that he knocked it over, pulling down half the flue pipe.

As the smoke from four gunshots drifted through the saloon, only the sheriff and Falcon, of the four original participants, were still standing. Both were holding smoking pistols in their hands, and they looked at each other warily.

"I thank you for taking a hand in this, mister," the sheriff said. "Most folks would have stayed on the sidelines."

"Yeah, well, I didn't really have that much choice in the matter," Falcon said.

The sheriff chuckled and nodded. "I guess you didn't at that," he said. He put his pistol away.

Falcon reholstered his own gun.

"Can I buy you a drink?" the sheriff asked.

Falcon looked pointedly at his beer mug, which now lay empty on the floor where he had dropped it when the shooting began.

"I guess I could use a new one at that," Falcon said.

"Two beers," the sheriff said.

The barkeep, who had dived to the floor behind the bar when the shooting started, now stood up, drew two beers, and put them on the bar.

"Thanks," Falcon said, taking a swallow of his beer.

"The name is Calhoun," the sheriff said as he lifted his own beer to his lips. "Titus Calhoun."

"Glad to meet you, Sheriff. I'm Falcon MacCallister."

Upon hearing Falcon's name, Sheriff Calhoun coughed and sprayed beer. Slamming his beer down on the bar, he reached for his pistol, only to find his holster was empty.

"Are you looking for this?" Falcon asked, holding the sheriff's pistol.

Seeing that Falcon had his gun, the sheriff put his hands up.

"Put your hands down, Sheriff," Falcon said. He put the pistol back in the sheriff's holster. "Whatever you think you might have on me, it's wrong. I'm not wanted anywhere."

"I . . . I reckon, under the circumstances, I've got no cause not to believe you," the sheriff said.

"Good. Now, maybe you can tell me about these two men we just had a run-in with."

"That one's Rollie Kofax," Sheriff Calhoun said, nodding toward the one he had shot. He looked over toward the stairs where the other man lay, half on the stairs and half off. "The one you shot was Willy Cardis. I just got word today that they was the ones that held up a stagecoach last week, over near Perdition. There was three of 'em, but Gilly Cardis got hisself caught."

"Gilly Cardis? You mean the two brothers' names were Willy and Gilly?" Falcon asked.

Sheriff Calhoun nodded. "They was twins," he said. "And I don't expect Gilly's goin' to be none too happy to hear that his brother got shot. I'd say it's a good thing he's in jail right now; otherwise, you'd probably wind up havin' another gunfight on your hands."

"Yeah," Falcon said drolly. "Seems like just about everyone I've ever run across had a brother somewhere. And those brothers all want to make things square."

"What are you doin' in Picacho, Mr. MacCallister? That is . . . if you don't mind my askin'."

"I don't mind at all," Falcon said. "I have some property down around Oro Blanco, I was just down seeing to it."

Sheriff Calhoun shook his head and clucked quietly. "That's not a place that's

15

too healthy to be right now. What with the Indian problem and all."

Falcon finished his beer. "Let me buy this round," he said. "That is, if you'd care for another."

"Don't mind if I do," Calhoun said.

"There's no Indian trouble now," Falcon said. "I had a nice meeting with Keytano and . . ."

Calhoun snapped his fingers and smiled broadly. "I know where I heard your name now," he said. "You and Mickey Free brought in Naiche a few years back, didn't you?"

"Yes."

"And Keytano? You had a . . . I believe you called it a nice meeting . . . with Keytano?"

"Yes," Falcon said.

Calhoun chuckled, and shook his head. "Only someone like you could call a meeting with Keytano nice."

"Keytano is a good man," Falcon said. "He's a man of honor, and I like men of honor."

Falcon finished his second beer, then set the empty mug down. He glanced toward the two dead men, who had been dragged to the back of the room and covered with a tarpaulin.

"I don't have to stick around for any kind of an inquest, do I?" he asked.

Calhoun shook his head. "No, but I'm sure there's a reward for Cardis. If you wait around a couple of days, I can get it approved and get the money to you."

"Do you have a volunteer fire department in town?" Falcon asked.

"Yes," Calhoun replied, puzzled as to why Falcon would ask about that.

"Give any reward money I might have to the volunteer fire department," he said. "I've never known one anywhere that couldn't use a little extra money."

The sheriff nodded. "You're right about that, Mr. MacCallister, and I'll do that for you," he said. "Speaking for the town, I'll tell you that we are grateful."

Falcon stuck out his hand for a handshake. "I need to get down to the depot to make arrangements to catch the train," he said. "Maybe I'll see you again sometime."

"It would be my pleasure," Sheriff Calhoun said.

"Who is that fella MacCallister anyway, Sheriff?" the bartender asked when Falcon left the saloon.

"He is the kind of man people tell tall stories about, Sam," Sheriff Calhoun replied. "Only in Falcon MacCallister's case,

17

they're all true."

When Falcon arrived in MacCallister the next afternoon, he stopped by the post office to pick up his mail. One of his letters was from his brother, Andrew, in New York, asking him again why he didn't just cash in everything and come to New York.

Falcon chuckled as he read the letter. He knew it was more than just brotherly love that made Andrew invite him. Despite his footloose life, Falcon was the wealthiest of all his siblings.

The other letter was from Conrad Kohrs.

Falcon held the letter for a moment or two before he opened it, wondering what the wealthiest cattle baron in America wanted with him.

Two

A rat, its beady eyes alert for danger, darted out from one of the warehouses onto the dank boards of the pier. Finding a piece of sodden bread, it picked up its prize, then darted back to the safety of its hole. Falcon MacCallister stood on the same pier, looking out over San Francisco Bay. He pulled the collar of his coat up against the damp chill air as he listened to a bell buoy clanging out in the harbor, its syncopated ringing notes measuring the passage of night. From somewhere close by a bosun's pipe sounded a shipboard signal, incomprehensible to landlubbers but fully understood by the ship's crew.

Gossamer tendrils of fog lifted up from the water and swirled around the pilings and piers so that the steel girders and wire cables of the dock's loading cranes became ethereal tracings. Long gray fingers of vapor had San Francisco trapped in its grasp.

There was no breeze.

The gaslights of the streetlamps were dimmed and all sound was deadened by the heavy blanket. There was a dreamlike quality to the scene that made it hard to distinguish fantasy from reality. Figures moved along the streets and sidewalks, but they were no more than apparitions gliding through the fog, appearing then disappearing as if summoned and dismissed by some prankish wizard.

Falcon was in San Francisco to take delivery of a horse for Conrad Kohrs. But it wasn't just any horse; it was a very special horse, bred by King Abdul Aziz of Arabia.

"A king's horse have I bought and for it a king's ransom have I paid," Kohrs said in the letter he had sent to Falcon.

Kohrs chose Falcon as his emissary, not only because the well-known cattle baron was Falcon's friend, but also because he knew Falcon would be coming to Montana to attend the Montana Stockgrowers' Association meeting.

The horse had been brought to America on board the *Sea Dancer,* a tall ship that plied the Pacific Ocean. Because of the value of the horse, it was shipped under special circumstances, not sharing a stall with other horses, but enjoying a private suite, constantly looked after by its own groomsmen.

Falcon had made arrangements to take delivery of the horse even before dawn because he intended to put it on the morning train.

The *Sea Dancer* lay at anchor alongside pier number seven, flaunting its half-naked dancing-girl figurehead, the long, sleek, gold-gilded black hull glistening in its own running lights. Someone was standing on the dock alongside the ship as Falcon approached. The man was wearing a dark peacoat and a billed cap. The sleeves of the coat, as well as the bill of the cap, were decorated with gold braid.

"Captain MacTavish?" Falcon asked.

"Aye, Captain Sean MacTavish at your service," the sailor answered. "And you would be Falcon MacCallister, I take it?"

"Yes."

"Well, 'tis a fine horse my old friend Connie is getting," Captain MacTavish said.

Falcon chuckled. "Connie?"

"Aye, it was Connie we called him when he sailed with us," MacTavish said. "I was a midshipman when first we met." MacTavish chuckled. "Connie and I went ashore in Calais. Ahh, the French girls. We were just boys, mind you, but we'd been around the

21

world a time or two, so we were pretty worldly for our age. But it turns out the captain didn't think so. We got a caning we did, the both of us."

MacTavish paused before he spoke again. "But the French girls . . . ah . . . the French girls. I tell you true, 'tis three canings I would have taken for the lessons those French girls taught us." The captain turned toward the ship.

"Mr. Peabody!" he called.

"Aye, Cap'n," a voice returned from the deck.

"Land His Highness."

"Aye, aye, sir."

MacTavish turned back to Falcon. "I don't know what Connie will call the horse, but we've been calling him His Highness, for true it is that he lived better than anyone did on the voyage, myself included."

A wide gangplank was lowered from the side of the ship; then a sailor came down the plank, leading the horse. Falcon walked over to examine the animal when it reached the dock.

The horse had a distinctive muscular profile with large, lustrous, wide-set eyes on a broad forehead, small, curved ears, and large, efficient nostrils. Falcon whistled softly.

"He's quite a beauty, isn't he?" MacTavish said.

"Yes, he is."

" 'Twas said, when we took him aboard, that he was the king's favorite."

"Then why did the king part with him?"

" 'Tis said he wanted the bloodline to start in America," MacTavish said. He rubbed his hands together. "Well, m'boy'o, 'tis your responsibility now. Do give Connie my best."

"I'll do that," Falcon said.

"You sure he's pickin' up that horse this early, Dingo?" Cyrus asked. "Hell, it ain't even light yet."

"Yeah, He's gettin' him early so he can put 'im on the eight o'clock train."

"How do you know this?"

" 'Cause I met some fella off the ship that brung the horse over," Dingo said. "We was drinkin' together. He got drunk and the next thing you know, he was tellin' me about this here ten-thousand-dollar horse."

"You know that's a load of bullshit," Cyrus said. "There ain't no horse worth ten thousand dollars. And even if there was, who would you find to pay you that much for it?"

"This here horse is worth that much. He's

one of them special breed of horses that kings and the like have," Dingo said. "But we ain't goin' to try and get that much money for him. If we sell him for five hunnert dollars, well, that's five hunnert we don't have now."

"Yeah, well, somethin' else we don't have now is the horse," Cyrus said.

"Shhh," Dingo said. "Here he comes now."

Falcon was riding a rental horse, and leading the Arabian. Suddenly, there was a flash in the darkness and the sound of a gunshot echoed back from the line of warehouses. Falcon felt the impact of the bullet as it hit his horse; then the horse went down under him.

"I got 'im!" Dingo said.

"You got the horse," Cyrus corrected.

"It's the same thing."

"No, it ain't the same thing. If you hadn't kilt the horse, we could'a had both of the horses. You should'a aimed at the rider."

"I *was* aimin' at the rider," Dingo said. "Come on, let's check him out."

The two men moved up cautiously toward the fallen horse. They could see the rider lying, perfectly motionless, pinned to the ground by the horse that was on his leg.

"I think he's dead," Dingo said.

"What makes you think he's dead?"

"Look at the way he's lyin' there. His eyes is open, but they ain't movin'. He don't look like he's breathin'."

"Check 'im out, Dingo. See if he's dead," Cyrus said.

Holding his pistol beside him, Dingo leaned over the motionless form of the rider, then reached out with his other hand to check for a pulse.

Falcon remained still until Dingo got close enough. Then, reacting quickly, Falcon reached up and grabbed the assailant's gun, jerking it away cleanly.

"What the hell?" Dingo shouted, taking a step back in surprise.

Falcon's leg only appeared to be trapped. In fact, it was under the soft belly of the horse, so it was very easy for him to pull it out.

"Shoot 'im, Cyrus, shoot 'im!" Dingo shouted.

Falcon sat up then and cocked his pistol. The deadly double click of the sear engaging the cylinder sounded exceptionally loud in the still morning darkness.

"I wouldn't listen to Dingo if I were you, Cyrus," Falcon said.

"Dingo, the son of bitch knows our names," Cyrus said. "How does he know our names?"

Falcon chuckled. Were these two so dumb that they didn't even realize they had just given him their names?

"Unbuckle the gun belt," Falcon said to Cyrus.

"You goin' to shoot us, mister?" Cyrus asked, his voice cracking with fear.

"I might," Falcon said. "I don't have time to take you to jail."

"If you're goin' to shoot someone, shoot him," Cyrus said. "This here wasn't my idea."

"Shut up, Cyrus. We was both in on this."

"But you was the one that come up with it," Cyrus said. "You said there was this here real valuable horse and we could steal him and sell him. That's what you said."

Falcon chuckled. "Were you going to share in the money, Cyrus?"

"Well, yeah," Cyrus said.

"Well, there you go then. You are as guilty as Dingo."

"Yeah," Dingo said. "There you go, you're as guilty as me. So he's goin' to shoot both of us."

Falcon sighed. He really didn't have time to take them to jail, and he had no intention of shooting either one of them, even though they were damn near too dumb to live. But he couldn't just let them go. Then he got an idea.

"Take off your clothes," he said.

"What?"

"Take off your clothes, both of you."

"Are you sayin' you want us to strip down to our long handles?" Cyrus asked.

Falcon shook his head. "No, I'm saying I want you to strip down to the skin. I want both of you butt naked."

"Mister, I ain't a' goin' to do that," Dingo said.

"All right," Falcon said. "Cyrus, you strip while I kill Dingo."

"Yes, sir, I'll strip," Cyrus said. "You go ahead and shoot him."

"No, wait!" Dingo said, holding his hands out in front of him. "Don't shoot, don't shoot! What's the matter with you, Cyrus, tellin' him to shoot me?"

"Well, if you won't take offen your clothes like he said," Cyrus said as he pulled off one of his boots.

"All right, all right, I'll strip," Dingo said.

Lifting up first one foot, then the other, the men started removing their boots.

"Mister, this ain't natural," Dingo said. "It ain't right, you makin' us strip like this."

"It wasn't right for you to shoot at me either."

"I didn't shoot you, I shot the horse."

"But you said you was shootin' at him," Cyrus said.

"Cyrus, will you shut up?"

A moment later, both men stood naked, shivering in the morning chill.

"Now what?" Dingo asked.

"Take your clothes over to the edge of the dock and drop them in the water." Falcon shifted his gun to his left hand, then threw the gun he had grabbed from Dingo toward the bay. It made a little splashing sound as it went into the water. "Drop your holsters in there too."

Glaring in anger, the two men scooped up their clothes, then padded barefoot across the board dock. They looked toward him in one last, fruitless appeal. He waved his gun to tell them to go through with it.

Both men dropped clothes and holsters into the water, then looked back at Falcon.

"Now what?" Dingo said.

Falcon shrugged. "Now nothing," he said. "I'm through with you. You can go on your way."

"Go on our way? Where are we going to go, naked like this?"

"I don't care," Falcon said. "Just get out

28

of my sight. I've never seen anything uglier than you two naked jay-birds."

Dingo and Cyrus hurried away, disappearing into the morning gloom. They continued arguing with each other and Falcon could hear them, even after he could no longer see them.

Falcon laughed out loud, then looked at the Arabian, who through it all had stood quietly.

"Well, horse," Falcon said. "I hadn't planned on riding you, but I guess I've got no choice now. We've got a train to catch."

Falcon took the saddle from the rental horse, put it on the Arabian, then mounted and rode off. Even in a ride like this, he could tell that this was some horse. Maybe not a ten-thousand-dollar horse, but it was some horse.

Lowell Spivey, the guard at the maximum-security blockhouse of the Yuma Territorial Prison, settled back in his chair and looked up at the clock. It was two-thirty in the morning. Spivey had just switched to the night shift and was having a hard time adjusting to it. He was tired and wanted to go to sleep. And though he could close his eyes and grab a quick nap in the chair, it was frowned upon.

"Hey, Spivey?" one of the prisoners called.

"What do you want?" Spivey answered.

"You better come have a look at Cardis."

"What's wrong with him?"

"I don't know, but he's back there moanin' like he's hurtin' real bad."

"It can wait till mornin'," Spivey replied.

"Then if you ain't goin' to do nothin' about it, at least come back here and tell 'im to shut up. He's keepin' the rest of us awake."

"Yeah," one of the other prisoners shouted. "Or open up his cell and let one of us shut 'im up."

A couple of the other prisoners laughed.

With a sigh, Spivey got up, opened the outer door, and walked down the cell-flanked corridor toward the cell that was Cardis's. When Spivey reached Cardis's cell, he saw the prisoner doubled up on his bunk, both arms wrapped across his stomach.

"What is it?" Spivey asked. "What's wrong with you?"

"I think it was somethin' I et at supper," Cardis grunted.

"Everybody else ate the same thing," Spivey said. "How come you're the only one complaining?"

"Maybe 'cause I'm the only one that got sick," Gilly Cardis replied.

"Yeah, well, try and keep quiet, will you?" Spivey asked. "You're keeping the others awake."

"I'll try," Cardis said. Suddenly he gasped, and grabbed his stomach again.

"All right, all right," Spivey said, pulling out the keys. "Come on, I'll take you to the dispensary so the doc can take a look at you."

"Thanks," Cardis said.

Spivey put the key in the lock, but before he opened the door, he looked at Cardis.

"Don't just sit there, you know what to do."

"Yeah, I know what to do," Cardis answered, though he didn't change from his doubled-over position.

"Well, do it, Cardis, I'm not going to stand here all night," Spivey said.

"Don't get all in a huff, I'm doin' it," Cardis grunted.

Cardis stood up and leaned against the wall. Spivey walked over to him, then pulled one of Cardis's arms into position and started to cuff his hands behind his back. Cardis let out a cry of pain. "I can't get my arms behind me," he grunted. "It hurts my gut too much."

"You know the rules. If I let you out of your cell at any time other than when it's

31

authorized, you have to have your hands cuffed."

"Can't you cuff 'em in front?"

Spivey hesitated for a long moment; then he sighed. "All right, I'll cuff 'em in front. But I ain't supposed to be doin' this, so don't give me any trouble."

Cardis held his hands together in front while Spivey put the manacles on him. The manacles were held together by a short length of chain so that when his wrists were bound, Cardis could hold his hands about twelve inches apart.

"Okay, tough guy, let's go," Spivey said. "You lead the way; you know where the dispensary is." He pushed Cardis roughly to get him started.

Procedure called for Spivey to inform one of the other guards anytime he took a prisoner from the cell, but he didn't see any of the other guards around.

"Collins," Spivey said to the prisoner who had told him about Cardis, "if you see Kane, tell 'im I took Cardis to the dispensary, will you?"

"Yeah, I'll tell 'im," Collins called back from the dark of his cell.

"All right, you wanted to go to the dispensary, let's go," Spivey said, poking Cardis with his nightstick.

"I ain't the one asked to go to the dispensary," Cardis said.

"No, you didn't. You was just gonna lie in there an' moan all night. Come on, let's go." He jabbed Cardis with his nightstick again, this time in the small of the back, hard enough to make the killer gasp.

They left the cell block and stepped out into the still, dark night. Cardis looked up at the sky. It was a desert-clear night, with stars so bright that he felt as if he could almost reach up and pull one down.

Cardis's eyes scanned the prison yard, going immediately to the guard positions on top of the wall. None of the guards were watching. He grasped the chain with his fingers and waited until he and Spivey were around the corner from the dispensary.

"Ohh!" he suddenly said, stopping and bending over, almost as if he were about to fall.

"What is it now?" Spivey asked, the tone of his voice reflecting his irritation with the prisoner.

"My belly's on fire," Cardis gasped.

"Well, the quicker you get to the dispensary, the quicker you can get somethin' done about it," Spivey said, taking a step closer to him. "Come on, let's go."

Whirling around quickly, and using the

small length of chain as a club, Cardis hit the guard and Spivey went down.

Cardis rifled through Spivey's pockets until he found the key. Then, unlocking the cuffs, he put on Spivey's hat and coat and started toward the front gate, walking as confidently as if he fully expected the guard to open the gate for him.

Cardis's bold move paid off. The guard at the gate barely looked up from his newspaper as he pulled the lever to unlock the gate. With a little wave, Cardis, who kept his head down for the whole time, simply stepped through. He continued to walk slowly until he disappeared into the dark; then he broke into a run.

THREE

"Miles City," the conductor called, coming through the car. "Next stop is Miles City."

Falcon was napping with his arms folded across his chest, his knees propped up on the seat back before him and his black hat tipped down over his eyes.

"Miles City, Mr. MacCallister," the conductor said.

"Thanks," Falcon said, sitting up and looking through the window as the train slowed for the station.

Miles City, Montana, got its start when Colonel Nelson A. Miles was dispatched by Secretary of War James Donald Cameron to build a cantonment where the Tongue River flowed into the Yellowstone. Colonel Miles, who was later to be General Miles, was sent into the territory to make a military response to the Battle of the Little Big Horn. His assignment was to protect settlers and freight wagons as they passed through the

35

fertile Yellowstone Valley. The cantonment was constructed in the fall of 1876, and by spring of 1877, a town had sprung up two miles away to provide rest and recreation for the soldiers.

Within the year, the cantonment moved to higher ground, becoming Fort Keogh, and the town followed, picking up lock, stock, and whiskey barrel and moving to the present location. Within a year after its move, the town was clearly established, boasting a population of more than two hundred citizens and growing larger every day.

A post office was established, and the town was officially named Miles City, after Colonel Miles. Having the town named after him didn't improve its relations with the military commander, though. Nelson Miles was a temperance man and he resented having a town "founded upon depravity and the consumption of whiskey" named for him.

Miles City quickly became known as a "hoorah" town full of soldiers and cowboys, gamblers and barkeepers, and the "soiled doves" who provided much of the town's economic backbone. With the arrival of the railroad, however, the complexion of the town changed from one of debauchery to one of honest commerce. It became the center of the cattle industry in an area that the cattlemen called the "Northern Range."

In its new manifestation, it served as the headquarters city for the Montana Stockgrowers' Association. The city was the home of the annual MSA meeting, and it was for that reason that Falcon had come to Montana, though Kohrs's horse, which was in a private stock car attached to this very train, was certainly a strong secondary reason.

At least 175 other ranchers would be attending, from the heavyweight local cattle growers, to the out-of-territory cattle barons such as John Clay, Granville Stuart, Pierre Wibaux, the Marquis de Mores, and others.

In addition to the cattle barons, the railroads, stockyards, and meatpacking plants were represented as well, sending their own high-ranking officers to mingle with the cattlemen. They had come to make plans for the roundup and cattle shipments coming up in the spring, as well as to treat themselves to a big convention celebration.

Falcon knew that during the annual meeting, the town of Miles City would more than double in population, and when the hotels and boardinghouses ran out of rooms, many of the attendees from the smaller ranches would put up tents and camp just outside of town. He didn't have to worry about that, though, because he had already booked a room at the MacQueen House, the town's largest and most elegant hotel.

Falcon was standing on the lowest step by the time the train squeaked to a stop at the depot. The depot platform was crowded with people who had come to meet the train, most because they were welcoming guests for the upcoming festivities, but almost as many were there simply because the arrival of the train was always an event.

An enterprising elixir salesman was taking advantage of the crowd, holding up a bottle as he made his pitch.

"Men, do you suffer from nervous debility, exhausted vitality, seminal weakness, lost manhood, impotency, paralysis, and all the terrible effects of self-abuse and youthful follies, such as loss of memory, lassitude, nocturnal emission, aversion to society, dimness of vision, or noises in the head? Then you should take Dr. Mintie's Kidney Remedy and Restorative. For just twenty-five cents the bottle, I guarantee that you will be cured. And this guarantee is backed by no less an authority than Rutherford B. Hayes, the President of the United States."

"Mister, are you telling us that the President of the United States suffers from all those things?"

"Although the President is a teetotaler now, it is a well-guarded secret that he had a misspent youth," the elixir salesman explained. He held up a bottle. "And only the marvelous curative powers of this elixir have saved him from the effects of those youthful indiscretions."

"You should get some of that, George," Falcon heard a woman say. "If the President of the United States uses it, it must be good."

"I'll take a bottle," George said.

"One won't be enough. You'll need four at least. But I'll tell you what I'll do. For you, five bottles for a dollar."

Chuckling, and shaking his head, Falcon walked away. Near the back of the platform, he saw a man holding up a sign.

FALCON MACCALISTER

Falcon didn't go to him right away. He had made a lot of enemies in his travels, and it would be very foolish to expose himself without first making certain that everything was on the up-and-up. After a moment or two of perusing the situation, he walked up to him.

"I'm Falcon MacCallister," he said.

"Mr. MacCallister, I'm Bert Rowe," the

cowboy said. "Did you bring Mr. Kohrs's horse?"

Falcon nodded. "He's in the stock car."

"Good. Mr. Kohrs asked me to pick it up for him."

"Where is Mr. Kohrs?"

"He sends his regards, and says he'll be coming in town first thing tomorrow morning," the young cowboy said. "He said he would get a message to you."

"All right," Falcon said. "Come on, we'll get the horse."

Falcon helped Bert Rowe take possession of the horse, then watched as the cowboy rode off, leading the Arabian. After that, Falcon made arrangements to have his luggage sent to his room at the MacQueen House. Then he wandered through the crowded streets of the town until he wound up at Duffey's.

A sign behind the bar invited customers to TEST THE SKILL OF OUR BARTENDER BY REQUESTING A MIXED DRINK.

The bartender was wearing a brocaded vest over a clean white shirt and a dark blue tie. A watch, with a massive gold chain, stretched across his chest, while a pair of garters held up his sleeves.

"What can I get you, sir?" the bartender asked.

"A beer," Falcon answered.

"Are you sure you wouldn't want to try one of our mixed drinks?" he asked. "They are my specialty."

"And I'm sure you do a great job mixing them," Falcon said. "But a beer will be fine."

"Very good, sir."

When the beer was brought to him, Falcon turned his back to the bar to survey the room. Half-a-dozen bar girls were moving from table to table, laughing, joking, and flirting with the men. Like everything else about this establishment, the girls were first class. They were all pretty, and none of them had the hard-worn look of dissipation that was so common among most girls of their trade.

One of them, a dark-haired girl with flashing brown eyes, saw him looking at her. Smiling prettily, she came over to talk to him.

"Are you in town for the stockgrowers' convention?" she asked.

"I am," Falcon answered. "Can I buy you a drink?"

The girl smiled. "Why, thank you," she said. "Karl," she called to the bartender. "Would you make me a daiquiri?"

"I'd be honored to, Miss Lucy," the bartender replied.

"Karl isn't just any bartender. He is qualified to make mixed drinks," Lucy explained.

"So I gather by the sign," Falcon said.

"It's very busy in here tonight," Lucy said.

Falcon had a drink with Lucy, enjoying her company and sense of humor. Though she let it be known by subtle hints that she would welcome the opportunity to take him to her crib, she wasn't overt about it, so he didn't have to come right out and refuse the invitation. Finally, she realized that he wasn't a potential customer, so she smiled, then took her leave, mingling quickly and easily with the other patrons of the saloon.

After another beer and a few hands of poker, Falcon folded his cards and declared that he was going to have dinner.

"I'm new to the town," he said. "Do any of you have a recommendation?"

"You could eat at MacQueen's, of course," one of the players said. "The hotel does have a dining room, and quite a good one."

"Yes, I assumed it did," Falcon said. "And I'll probably be taking many of my meals there. But I'd like to try somewhere else tonight."

"In that case, you can't beat Little Man's."

"Little Man's?"

"Little Man Lambert. The meals aren't

fancy, but they are good."

"Thanks," Falcon said. "Open chair," he announced to anyone who might want to sit in the game. Then, as another customer took Falcon's abandoned chair, he left the saloon and walked down to Little Man Lambert's Café.

Little Man Lambert's was not a very large place. In fact, it was quite small, but it was very crowded, which, Falcon deduced, was a testimony to the quality of the food. Directed to a seat in the back corner where he shared the table with another diner, he picked up the menu. Suddenly he saw a roll flying by, and looking up in surprise, saw a man standing at the kitchen door, throwing rolls about the room.

"What is this?" Falcon asked.

His dining partner chuckled. "Throwed rolls is what Little Man is famous for," he said. "The dining room is too crowded for him to walk around, so he makes fresh rolls, then comes out and throws them to whoever wants one."

"How does he know who wants one?"

"You want one?"

"Yes."

"Hold your hand up in a catching position."

Amused by it all, Falcon held his hand

up. He no sooner got his hand in position than a roll came sailing across the café floor, hitting him squarely in the hand. He caught it easily.

"He's very good at that," Falcon said with a smile.

"He ought to be. He throws about one hundred rolls a day," his table partner told him.

After Gilly Cardis escaped prison, his first order of business was to get some money. In order to do that, in the middle of the night he broke into the only place available on such short notice, a small general store just outside Yuma. He stole a change of clothes, thirty-one dollars, and a Colt .44. A few minutes later he stole a horse from a private barn. He rode the horse to the nearest stagecoach way station, but about one mile before he got there, he let the horse go. That was just in case someone might have recognized the horse.

He walked to the way station and stopped at the pump outside, then began pumping, holding his hand over the spout of the pump, letting the water build up so he could lean down and suck it in through his lips.

The station attendant came out to see him.

"You come here without a horse?" he asked.

Cardis nodded. "He stepped in a prairie-dog hole about five or six miles back," he said. "I had to put him down."

"Sorry," the attendant said. "I know that's always a hard thing to do."

"Can I buy a stage ticket here?"

"Sure can. Where would you like to go?"

"To the nearest place I can catch a train, I reckon."

"That would be Adonde," the attendant said. "You'll get there in time to catch the seven o'clock train tonight."

"Good."

Cardis had not planned much beyond his escape from prison. Once he got to a rail-road station, he planned to buy a ticket to Phoenix, because he hoped to meet his brother there. He wasn't sure that's where Willy would be, but that was where the three of them had planned to go after the stage robbery.

The robbery had gone bad. They got no money, and Gilly was shot and captured. At least his brother and Kofax got away.

"Come on in and I'll sell you a ticket," the attendant said. "That'll cost you three dollars. The stage should be here within half an hour or so and they'll be stoppin' for their lunch. You want lunch, it'll cost you an extra quarter."

Cardis had not eaten since the prison supper the night before. The excitement of the escape, and his need to get away, had kept him from thinking about food, but now that the station attendant mentioned it, he realized just how hungry he was.

"Lunch sounds good," Cardis said. "I'm so hungry I could eat a horse."

The station attendant laughed. "Well, sometimes these stringy old longhorns can taste like a horse," he said. "But I promise you, it is beef."

Cardis was in the privy when he heard the trumpet blast signaling that the coach was arriving. Finishing quickly, he was out of the outhouse and standing on the front porch as the stage pulled in. The shotgun guard glanced toward him and held his gaze for so long that, for a moment, Gilly was afraid that he might have been recognized.

The shotgun guard spit a quid of tobacco just over the wheel as the coach creaked to a stop. Then, losing interest in whatever had held his attention during the long, piercing look, the guard put his weapon down, stood up, and stretched.

"Gray's Station," the driver called. "We'll

be here for half an hour. Food inside."

Half an hour later, the coach, now with a fresh team, was under way again. Besides Gilly, there were only two other passengers on the coach: a drummer, who slept through most of the trip, and an old man who wasn't very sociable. That was fine with Cardis, who would just as soon not talk to anyone anyway.

By the time the coach reached Adonde, the train was already standing in the station. Hurrying, he bought the cheapest ticket he could to Phoenix.

"Do you have any baggage to check through?" the ticket agent asked.

"No," Cardis said, taking the ticket and starting toward the track. "It's just me."

A woman, carrying two packages and a baby, was struggling to get onto the train. A boy of about six was with her. She glanced toward Cardis, hoping he would offer a hand, but rather than assist her, he stepped in front of her, got on the car, found a seat, and sat down.

Another male passenger, who was already on the train, saw the woman struggling with her load as she came into the car, and he jumped up quickly to help.

"Thank you," the woman said. She looked

47

at Cardis again, as if trying to make him feel embarrassed by the fact that he had not offered to help, but Cardis paid no attention to her.

The train car had hard wooden benches and smelled of kerosene, strange foods, and unwashed bodies, but Cardis wasn't a man of discriminating sensitivities, so none of it mattered. At the moment all Cardis was looking to do was to put as much distance between himself and the Yuma prison as he could, as fast as he could.

It was dark by the time the train got under way, and Cardis was tired and irritable as he sat on the unyielding wooden seat, staring into the darkness outside the train, looking at the little squares of yellow light that, projected by the passenger-car windows, were sliding alongside the track on the ground below. He was so lost in his own thoughts that he was totally oblivious to the sounds, sights, and smells of the car.

"Paper?"

"What?" Cardis replied gruffly, irritated at having been spoken to.

"I'm finished with this. I asked if you would like to read the paper," a man said, holding a paper toward Cardis.

"Nah, I don't want the paper," Cardis said grumpily. "I don't want to talk to no one neither."

"I'm sorry," the man apologized, pulling the paper away. "I had no wish to intrude."

Just as the man was withdrawing the paper, Cardis happened to see his brother's name.

"Hold it!" he said sharply, reaching for the paper. "Let me see that."

"Sure thing, mister."

Cardis held the paper under the kerosene lantern and folded the paper to the article that had caught his attention. The article read:

A DARING SHOOT-OUT!
Stagecoach Robbers Shot Dead In Saloon.
Reward to go to Volunteer Fire Brigade.

Two villains, Rollie Kofax and Willy Cardis, who had but recently tried their hands at robbing a stagecoach, came to Picacho recently. It is believed they were in Picacho in order to secure passage on a train, thus putting a great distance between themselves and their failed attempt to hold up the Perdition stagecoach.

Thinking they were safe in a small

town, the two men had not counted upon the valor of Sheriff Titus Calhoun, who, upon recognizing Rollie Kofax, addressed him with the intention of placing him under arrest. Kofax responded to the sheriff's demand by issuing a deadly challenge. He felt secure in doing this because he believed that his confederate, Willy Cardis, was in position to offer him a strategic advantage.

What neither Kofax nor Cardis took into consideration was the intervention of a good citizen. This good citizen confronted Cardis when he saw the villain aiming his pistol at the sheriff's back.

Cardis then turned his pistol toward the good citizen, not realizing that he was facing none other than the legendary Falcon MacCallister, a man whose speed and marksmanship with a pistol is legend throughout the West. Indeed, dime novels proliferate about the many exploits of Falcon MacCallister.

When the smoke cleared away, both Sheriff Calhoun and Falcon MacCallister were standing, while their recent adversaries lay mortally wounded upon the saloon floor. Falcon MacCallister, in keeping with his reputation as an out-

50

standing citizen, declined the two-hundred-and-fifty-dollar reward that was offered for Willy Cardis, suggesting that it be paid instead to the local volunteer fire brigade. MacCallister, it is believed, has returned to his home near Denver, Colorado.

Kofax had no known relatives and Willy Cardis's only known relative was his brother, who is currently serving a prison term in Yuma Territorial Prison. As a result of there being no interested parties to attend to their last rites, the two villains were buried without funeral or fanfare in the paupers' section of the local cemetery.

So, Cardis thought. This man Falcon MacCallister lives in Denver, Colorado, does he? Cardis had never been to Denver, but if that's where MacCallister was, that's where he was going. And as soon as he found MacCallister, he was going to kill him.

FOUR

It was dark by the time Falcon finished his dinner. Leaving the restaurant, he walked down to the MacQueen House, where he had taken a room for the night. As he passed through the lobby, he saw two well-dressed men arguing with the desk clerk.

"What do you mean you have no rooms?" one of the men was complaining. "Surely you knew that there was to be a big meeting here this week. You should have made arrangements for that."

"No, sir," the clerk replied. "*You* should have made arrangements for that. All those who have rooms tonight had the foresight to reserve them in advance."

"Well, just where you suggest we stay?"

"Many are camping just outside of town," the clerk said. "In fact, I think there are still some tents available for rent."

"Tents? Are you suggesting that I stay in a tent?" the man asked in a blustering fashion.

"I'm just saying that there may still be some tents available."

"I'll have you know, sir, that I own ten thousand acres of prime cattle land back in Idaho."

"That may well be, sir. But you aren't in Idaho," the clerk replied, maintaining his composure.

As Falcon climbed the stairs to his room, he passed out of earshot of the argument going on in the lobby.

Just before he went into his own room, he saw a very attractive young woman trying to make the key work in one of the other doors.

"Allow me," he said, stepping over and taking the key from her.

"Oh, thank you," the woman said. "I am so clumsy when it comes to such things."

Falcon opened the door for her, then slipped the key into the lock from the other side of the door.

"Just turn this when you get inside," he said. "It will secure your room."

"Thank you," the woman said again. "Good night."

"Good night."

Falcon let himself into his own room, then got ready for bed. It had been a long, tiring ride on the train for the last few days, so the bed felt very comfortable to him.

As he lay in bed, he could hear the sounds of the town at night . . . a playing piano, a woman's high-pitched laugh, a man's low-rumbling guffaw, and a couple of cowboys talking out on the street. Soon all the sounds blended and dimmed, and Falcon fell asleep.

When Falcon awakened the next morning, the sounds of the town were completely changed. Last night the sounds had been those of a town at play. This morning they were the sounds of commerce. Across the street the proprietor of the general store was sweeping his porch, and Falcon could hear the scratching of the broom straws against the weathered wood. He could also hear the sound of a building being erected: the back-and-forth rip of a saw, the banging of a hammer, the chatter of carpenters at work. A heavy wagon rolled by on the street, and from the nearby laundry he could hear the singsong chatter of the Chinese at work.

Using the pitcher and basin, Falcon washed his face and hands and shaved. Then he went downstairs to breakfast.

At the far end of the street from the Mac-Queen House, young Joey Mitchell was sitting on the floor in the back corner of a meeting room of the Montana Stockgrowers' Association, reading a dime novel entitled *Dingus McGee's Doom: Or, The Triumph of Falcon MacCallister.*

So absorbed was Joey in the vivid prose of his book that he scarcely noticed all the people coming and going, or milling about him. Although Joey was reading to himself, his lips were forming the words.

"Get ready to eat your supper in hell," the intrepid hero said as he turned his flashing blue eyes toward his adversary.

Throughout the West, these eight words have been made famous and, for more than one nefarious ne'er-do-well, they were the last bit of human communication he would ever hear.

As quick as thought, both men, each bound and determined to kill the other, made desperate and determined grabs for the weapons strapped to their side.

What happened next, dear reader, took less time than it takes to spin the yarn. For the bullet from our hero's gun did, upon entering the villain's heart, cause the ruffian to expire at the moment he fell.

So great was the intensity of the silence caused by the shooting, that one could have heard a pin drop. This hazardous adventure had taken place in the bar-room of the Bucket of Blood Saloon — the wildest of all the wild saloons in the even wilder town of Death Gap.

Then, falling upon the ears of all therein, came frightful words, spoken in a loud and dangerous voice.

"Let this be a lesson to any and all who would seek to best me, for seventy and more have fallen before my gun. Ha! Ha!"

Following those words, the barroom was filled with a wild peal of mirth. The laughter, as if echoing from the very chambers of the devil himself, chilled the blood of everyone who heard, so fearfully suggestive of a gunman's tri-umph it was. Not one man within the tavern made a move to discover the author of the laugh infernal, nor was such an effort necessary, for all knew who it was. Even Dingus McGee, who many believed to be the most dangerous of all the nefarious gunmen, assumed a grayish pallor as he heard the laughter of the avenger, and he moved not a step from where he was.

The avenger was a man known throughout the West as the greatest of all gunfighters — a man who, by the mere mention of his name, could cause the blood of outlaws and ne'er-do-wells to run cold. For he who had bested the ruffian that day, as he had bested so many other ruffians on so many other days, was the scourge of evildoers throughout the West. This valiant man, who was a champion to damsels in distress, a defender of the meek in despair, and a hero to young boys everywhere, was none other than the man some called the "Knight of the West." Yes, dear readers, it was Falcon Mac-Callister.

"Joey! Joey!" Fred Matthews called.

Standing quickly, Joey dog-eared the page he had been reading, then stuck the novel down inside the waistband of his trousers.

"I'm right here, Mr. Matthews," he called back, answering the summons of his employer.

"I have a delivery for you."

"Yes, sir."

"Run down to the MacQueen House and give this message to one of their guests. You'll probably find him in the hotel dining room having breakfast about now."

Joey took the note from Matthews, then looking at the name of the addressee, gasped. "Mr. Matthews, this says that this note is for Falcon MacCallister."

"So?" Matthews replied.

"Falcon MacCallister is a hero!" Joey said.

"You don't say."

"That's what the book says," Joey said. He patted the book at his waist. "The writer of the book says he is a genuine hero."

"Well, if it says in the book that he is a hero, then he must be a hero," Matthews said without enthusiasm. "Now, run along with you and deliver the message like I said."

"Yes, sir!" Joey said excitedly.

Joey was a messenger for the Montana Stockgrowers' Association. The MSA provided a service of exchanging messages between cattlemen and businessmen in and immediately around Miles City. Such service was faster than the mail, and more convenient than the telegraph. And while there was always enough business to keep Joey employed, it was particularly busy this week, because this was the week of the annual meeting.

Leaving the office, Joey ran to the far end of Palmer Street until he reached the Mac-Queen House. He stayed out front of the hotel dining room for just a moment until he was able to catch his breath. Then he stepped inside, where he was greeted by the headwaiter.

"Yes?" the man said.

"I'm delivering a message for a man named MacCallister," the messenger said.

"That would be Falcon MacCallister?" the headwaiter said.

"Yes," Joey replied. "Uh, is it the same one?"

"I beg your pardon?"

Joey showed the man the book he had been reading. "I mean, is it this Falcon MacCallister? Or is it just someone with the same name?"

The man chuckled. "How old are you, young man?"

"Seventeen."

"I can't believe that a seventeen-year-old would even have to ask that question. Have you never heard of Falcon MacCallister?"

"Yes, of course I have," Joey answered. "I've just been reading about him."

"I don't mean the claptrap you read in one of those penny dreadfuls. Most of that is just garbage. I'm talking about the real Falcon MacCallister. Have you never heard anything about him?"

"I . . . I guess not."

"Where have you been for all your life?"

"Baltimore," Joey said. "I just moved to

Miles City a few months ago."

"I see. Well, so that you don't get all confused by the fairy tales people write, let me tell you something about the real Falcon MacCallister. He is much more than those novels portray. There are many who say that he is one of the most accomplished men with a six-gun to ever roam the West. And if you ever take issue with that statement, I would suggest that you keep the notion to yourself. It is no surprise that he has become a character in storybooks, but believe me, no story in any of those books can ever match what he has done in real life.

"Now, do you still want to know if this Falcon MacCallister is the same one you have read about?"

"No, sir, not anymore," Joey said. "I know he is. I have a message to deliver to him. That is, if he is here in the restaurant."

"He is. That's him, back there," the head-waiter said, pointing to a man who was sitting alone at a table next to the window in the rear of the restaurant. The man was bareheaded, but a black hat, decorated with a turquoise-encrusted silver band, sat on the table beside him. He was wearing a tan, fringed, buckskin jacket with a crisp white shirt and a black string tie.

Joey hesitated.

"Go ahead," the headwaiter said. "I told you, that's Falcon MacCallister. That's the man you are looking for."

"I . . . uh . . . hate to disturb him while he is eating."

The man chuckled. "Don't worry, he probably won't shoot you in here."

"You're sure?"

"I'm sure."

Joey started toward Falcon's table.

"No, he's much too nice a man for that. He'll wait until he gets you outside," the headwaiter called out to him.

"What?" Joey gasped.

The man laughed out loud. "I'm teasing you, boy. Take him your message."

Joey walked back to Falcon's table. He stopped before he got there and stood for a moment, watching as Falcon, who was having a breakfast of steak and eggs, carved a piece from his steak.

"What's your name, son?" Falcon asked without looking up.

"What? Oh, uh, it's Joey."

Joey had not seen Falcon even so much as glance in his direction, so the question caught him by surprise.

"You have a message for me, Joey?"

"Yes, sir," Joey said. "It's from Mr. Conrad Kohrs."

"Ah, good, I was expecting that."

Joey didn't move.

"Well, are you going to give me the note? Or are you going to try to make me guess what it says?"

"I . . . uh . . . oh!" Joey said, realizing that he was still holding the note. He held it toward Falcon. "Yes, sir, of course I'm going to give you the note."

"Thanks," Falcon said.

Joey turned to leave.

"Wait," Falcon called.

Joey stopped. Had he done something wrong? Anxiously, he turned back toward Falcon.

"Here," Falcon said, handing Joey a fifty-cent piece.

Joey's eyes grew wide in surprise and appreciation. It was not unusual for him to receive a tip from someone whenever he delivered a message, but most of his tips were a penny, sometimes a nickel, and only very rarely a dime. A fifty-cent tip was the largest tip he had ever received, and that was even going back to his days working as a Western Union delivery boy when he still lived in Baltimore.

"Oh, Mr. MacCallister, I almost forgot," Joey said, taking the book from where he had stuck it down in his pants. "Would you sign your autograph on this book for me?"

Falcon looked at the book and chuckled. "What for?" he asked. "I've never even heard of anyone who called himself Dingus McGee."

"I just want your autograph is all," Joey said. "Oh, and, would you put 'Get ready to eat supper in hell' by your name?"

"Why, boy? Do you want to eat your supper in hell?"

"What? No, sir," Joey said. "But, uh, it's what you always say just before you shoot a bad man."

"Is it now?" Falcon asked.

"Yes, sir. I know that because that's what it says in this book."

"I see," Falcon said with a little chuckle.

Falcon had never used that line in his life, but Joey wasn't the first person to point out to him that the dime novels reported that he always said that just before shooting someone. Falcon had long since given up refuting it, so he signed the book just as Joey requested, and was rewarded with a broad smile from the boy.

"Shall I wait to take a message from you?" Joey asked.

"I don't know, let me read this one," Falcon said, opening the note.

Falcon —
For the safe delivery of my beautiful horse,
I thank you. I look forward to visiting with
you while you are in town for the MSA
meeting.
> Yours respectfully,
> Conrad Kohrs

Falcon looked up at Joey. "I assume, Joey, that like all good messengers, you have a tablet and pencil?"

"Yes, sir," Joey said, producing the items.

Falcon scrawled one quick line.

It will be my pleasure.

He handed the note to Joey, who, with a quick nod, darted off to deliver it.

After breakfast, Falcon went out onto the street to join the others who were beginning to gather for the festivities. There were several soldiers in town, not only those who were enjoying a three-day pass from the post, but also those who were in town to participate in the parade.

The military band from Fort Keogh led off the parade, followed by a mounted unit of the Fifth Cavalry. That was followed by the MSA officers and their ladies, riding in highly polished carriages, then more than one hundred cowboys tiding on spirited ponies, sometimes darting to the head of the column, sometimes darting to the rear, whooping loudly and waving their hats as they did so.

The business meeting took place at the Miles City roller-skating rink and civic center. In addition to the several cattlemen who spoke, there were officers from the railroad who discussed shipping costs, stockyard and feeder-lot owners and managers talking holding-pen fees, and representatives from the meatpacking industry who quoted this spring's going price for cattle.

One of the cattlemen, Moreton Frewen, raised his hand for permission to talk. Falcon smiled as the little man began to speak. Stories of Frewen's business ineptitude abounded, including one about him buying the same herd of cattle twice when the unscrupulous sellers merely ran the herd around a hill and brought them back to sell them as a second herd.

"Seems to me like you're paying much less this year," Moreton Frewen said.

"We are," the meatpacker said.

"Why?"

"You have to understand that, unlike you gentlemen, we must sell our product by the pound," the meat-packer explained. "And as this has been a particularly harsh winter, we anticipate that the cattle will weigh less; therefore, we will make less profit per head."

Falcon listened for a few minutes, then grew bored with the discussion and went out into the town. Although he was as wealthy as any of the cattle barons, he actually felt more akin to the cowboys who were bellied up four deep at the saloon bars, or sitting around poker tables. At one establishment, called Turner's Theater, scantily clad girls were cajoling cowboys into drinking wine at five dollars per bottle or, for a price, going upstairs with them.

Falcon teased and flirted with the young soiled doves, but that was as far as his association with them went. Several of the women tried to entice him into sampling some of the pleasure they had to offer, and one young lady even suggested that he could "see the elephant" for free. But like Lucy the night before, none of them were successful in their endeavors.

FIVE

After an afternoon of playing cards and visiting with the cowboys, Falcon returned to the MacQueen House, where that evening a dance was to be held in the commodious dining room.

"Mr. MacCallister?" the desk clerk said as he walked by.

"Yes?"

"I believe you had reserved a bath for six o'clock this evening?"

"Yes."

"An earlier reservation has been canceled, so you can have your bath at five o'clock, if you wish."

"Thanks, I'll just do that."

"Very good, sir," the clerk replied. "It will be Bathroom A."

At five o'clock, Falcon walked down to the bathrooms at the end of the hall, carrying with him his change of clothes. The doors to Bathrooms A and B were closed.

He opened the door marked A.

At the precise moment he opened the door, an exceptionally pretty woman was just stepping down into the bath. The woman was totally nude.

"Sir!" she said, shocked by his intrusion. Quickly, she put one arm across her breasts, and the other over the triangle of dark hair at the junction of her legs. It was the same woman he had helped with the lock to her room earlier.

Falcon glanced back toward the open door and saw that it was clearly marked A. "I apologize," he said. "I was told that I had Bathroom A at five o'clock."

By now the woman had restored some modesty, if not dignity, by slipping down into the tub.

"A?" she said.

"Yes," Falcon replied.

"Oh," the woman said. "I didn't know it made any difference. I too had my bath scheduled for this hour, and as I saw this door open and a hot bath drawn, I assumed it was for me."

Falcon saw the key sticking from the lock. "Perhaps if you had locked the door," he suggested.

"I . . . I seem to have a difficult time with those infernal locks and keys," she said. "As you may remember," she added.

So far Falcon had not left, and he was surprised to see that, rather than exhibiting anger, the woman was showing a bemused smile.

"Well, are you going to leave, sir? Or do you intend to join me in my bath?" she asked.

"Oh!" Falcon said. He touched the brim of his hat. "I'm sorry," he said. "Of course I will leave." He backed out of the room and closed the door. Opening the door to Bathroom B, he saw that it too had a bath drawn. Chuckling quietly, he closed the door, locked it, then disrobed and settled into the tub.

Half an hour later, feeling clean and refreshed, Falcon was returning to his room when heard a young woman call out in alarm.

"Who are you?" the woman's voice called from behind a closed door. "What are you doing in my room? Help me! Somebody help me!"

Falcon knew that this was the room of the woman he had encountered in the bath a short time earlier.

"You better shut up, Girly, if you know what's good for you," a low, raspy voice growled.

Pulling his gun, Falcon opened the door to the room. He saw the same young woman, obviously frightened, and he saw the cause of her fright. A man was in her room, tall, with dark eyes and a black, sweeping mustache. He had a dark, very visible scar on his left cheek. The open window behind him gave Falcon a hint as to how he had come into the room.

Although Falcon's entrance must have surprised the scar-faced intruder, he reacted quickly. Grabbing the woman, he pulled her to him, pointing his own gun at her head.

"Now, don't you go trying to be a hero, mister," the intruder said. "I think maybe you had better put your gun down and get out of here."

"No, I don't think so," Falcon said.

"I said put your gun down, mister. Do it now, or I'll kill her."

"I tell you what. You let the lady go, and I won't kill you," Falcon said.

Falcon's words surprised the intruder, and he blinked a couple of times. "What? What did you say?"

"I said let the lady go and I won't kill you," Falcon said.

The intruder laughed, a wild, humorless laugh. "Mister, are you crazy? Do you see that I'm pointing a gun at her?"

"Exactly," Falcon said. "And that's where you made your mistake."

"A mistake? You call this a mistake?"

"Oh, I do indeed. You see, you are pointing the gun at her, not me." Falcon pointed his pistol at the man's head and cocked it. "I, on the other hand, am pointing my gun right at you. I'm going to count to three; then I'm going to kill you."

"I warn you, mister, if you start counting, I plan to kill her when you get to two," the intruder said resolutely.

"And I will kill you when I get to three," Falcon said. "One . . . two . . ."

"Wait! No, stop! All right!" the intruder said, putting his gun down and backing away from the woman. "I've let her go, see? Don't shoot, don't shoot!" He put his hands in the air.

"So we meet again," the woman said, smiling a relieved smile at Falcon. "I don't believe we introduced ourselves at our previous meetings. I am Kathleen Coyle. And this time, I truly am pleased to meet you."

"My name is MacCallister. Falcon Mac-Callister."

"You're . . . you're Falcon MacCallister?" the intruder asked. He had obviously heard of Falcon.

"What are you going to do with him, Mr. MacCallister?"

"It's up to you," Falcon said. "I can take him to jail, or I can finish my count to three." He raised his pistol and cocked it.

"What? No! My God, Mr. MacCallister, no!" Kathleen shouted. "Don't kill him!"

Falcon sighed. "All right, if you say so. But it is tempting."

Kathleen smiled coquettishly. "You were so brave to come charging to my rescue. I feel as if I should repay you in some way."

"No repayment necessary."

"But I really should do something," Kathleen said. "I know. Suppose you let me take you to dinner tonight."

"I'm afraid I have dinner planned," Falcon said.

"Oh." Kathleen looked crestfallen.

"You could come to dinner with *me*," Falcon suggested. "It's the Stockgrowers' Association Dinner and Dance. You could be my guest."

"A dance?" Kathleen said, brightening. "Why, I would be very honored to be your guest tonight."

"I'll call for you at six-thirty," he said. He looked toward the intruder, who had been following the dialogue between the two with great interest.

"What are you looking at?" Falcon asked his prisoner.

"Why don't you let me go?" the prisoner replied. "I didn't do nothin'. I was just in the wrong room, that's all."

"You've got that right, mister," Kathleen said heatedly. "You were in *my* room."

"Miss Coyle," Falcon started.

"Please, call me Kathleen."

"Kathleen, you know you are going to have to come down to the jail and file a complaint against this man. Otherwise, they'll have no reason to charge him and they'll have to let him go."

"Oh, don't you worry about that," Kathleen said. "I'll file a complaint, all right."

"You got nothin' to complain about," the intruder said. "I didn't do nothin'."

"Come on, let's go," Falcon said to the intruder, emphasizing his order with a wave of his pistol.

"Six-thirty tonight?" Kathleen said as Falcon started to leave with the intruder. "You won't disappoint me now, will you?"

"I'll call for you," Falcon promised.

"What's your name?" Sheriff Foster asked the man Falcon brought to him. The sheriff

73

began looking through the dodgers on his desk.

"You ain't got no paper on me," the scar-faced prisoner replied.

"You don't mind if I look, do you?" The sheriff nodded toward the scar. "With a scar like that, it'll be easy enough to find out if I have anything on you."

"My name is Johnny. Johnny Purvis. Go ahead and look. You won't find nothin'."

After a quick perusal of the wanted posters, Sheriff Foster looked back at his prisoner. "All right, I don't have anything on you," he said. "So I'll just hold you for breakin' and enterin' and threatenin' to kill an innocent woman."

"I wasn't really goin' to kill her. I was just tryin' to get away. Besides, I wasn't doin' nothin'. I was just in the wrong room, that's all."

"I might believe you, Mr. Purvis, if you had a room at the hotel," Foster said. "But with all the wealthy cattlemen in town, there is no way a saddle bum like you would have a room."

"What about the woman?" Johnny asked. "She sure ain't no cattleman."

"Perhaps not, but she does have a room at the hotel, and you don't," Sheriff Foster said. He took a key down from the hook on the wall, then nodded toward the cells in the back of the room. "But, of course, you don't need to be worrying about a hotel room now. I've got a nice cell, just for you."

Music for the dance that evening was supplied by a six-piece orchestra. The ballroom was filled with women in butterfly-bright dresses who bobbed and weaved to the music as broaches and necklaces sparkled in the golden light of dozens of candelabras. The men were well turned out as well, in tuxedos and suits or, in the case of the officers from the fort, in blue-and-gold braid with dress sabers.

Falcon enjoyed his time with Kathleen, who told him that she was a performer. "I came here seeking employment at Turner's Theater," she said. She looked down at the table in embarrassment. "I thought I would be asked to sing, or perhaps do a few readings. I didn't know that the girls at Turner's Theater wore so few clothes while they were working or that, indeed, I would be expected to do private performances."

"Yes, the girls there do dress provocatively," Falcon said.

"Heavens, if I had thought you would see me in my room when I was so scandalously dressed, I would be much too embarrassed

75

to . . ." Suddenly Kathleen paused in mid-sentence, then put her hand over her mouth to cover a laugh. "How ironic of me to think such a thing, when your first sight of me was au naturel," she added.

"I should have knocked before opening the door," Falcon apologized.

"It isn't your fault. And what's done is done."

"Have you been a performer long?"

"Not too long," Kathleen said. "I know it is foolish of me, but it has always been my ambition to perform on the stage in New York."

"Not foolish at all. Have you ever been to New York?"

"No. But I know it must be wonderful."

"I don't know that I would call it wonderful, but it is interesting," Falcon said. "My brother and sister perform on the stage in New York."

"Your brother and sister?"

"Andrew and Rosanna MacCallister," Falcon said.

"Andrew and Rosanna MacCallister? Yes, yes, I have heard of them," Kathleen said. "You must be very proud to have such famous siblings."

"Yes," Falcon said. "I am proud of them."

■ ■ ■ ■

Falcon thought of his siblings. He could remember how, even before the war, they would entertain not just the family, but all the people of MacCallister Valley.

Everyone said then that they were good enough to be professionals, but no one really believed the twins would actually follow through with their ambitions. After all, MacCallister Valley was a long way from New York.

But follow through they did, and once Falcon went to New York to see them for the first time in many years.

Falcon MacCallister was not a man who was easily impressed, but it was hard not to be awed by New York. The streets were crowded with a steady-moving stream of conveyances of all kinds, from wagons to carriages to horse-drawn omnibuses. In addition, trains moved back and forth through the city, sometimes on elevated rails, sometimes on the ground.

"What do you think of our city, little brother?" Rosanna had asked.

"I'll be honest with you," Falcon replied. "I don't like it."

"You don't like it?" Andrew said. "How

can anyone not like New York? Why, this is the most exciting city in the whole world."

"It's too crowded," Falcon said.

"Of course it is crowded. It is a big city," Andrew said.

"Well, there you go. MacCallister is too crowded for me," Falcon said.

Rosanna and Andrew laughed.

"Andrew, were you and I ever such country bumpkins?" Rosanna asked.

"Surely not," Andrew said.

Falcon didn't say it out loud, but just as they wondered how he could be such a bumpkin, he wondered how they could be such dandies. If he hadn't known for a fact that they were his blood kin, no one would have been able to convince him of it.

"Goodness, you are miles away right now," Kathleen said.

Falcon smiled across the table at her. "Sorry," he said. "I was just thinking of my brother and sister."

"I would love to meet them sometime," Kathleen said. "How wonderful it would be to meet them in New York and tell them that I know their brother."

"I'm sure they would make you feel very welcome."

"Falcon," a man's voice said. "It is good

to see you, *mein freund.*" He paused when he saw Kathleen. "Oh, I'm sorry. You are with a woman and I do not wish to intrude."

The man who approached was a rather short, stout man with white hair, a broad face, large, expressive blue eyes, and a bushy beard that matched the hair in color and was squared off at the bottom.

"You are never an intrusion," Falcon said, standing and extending his hand. "I would like you to meet my friend, Kathleen. Kathleen, this is Conrad Kohrs."

Kathleen gasped and put her hand to her mouth. "*The* Conrad Kohrs? The great cattle baron?" she asked.

Kohrs laughed. "In my home country, one can only be a baron if one has inherited a title," he said. "A poor peasant boy like me could not be a baron. Here in America, I raise a few cows, and it is baron I have become. America is a wonderful country."

"Excuse me, Mr. Kohrs, but one hundred thousand head are not a few cows," Kathleen said.

"Oh? And have you been counting my cows, *fraulein?*" Kohrs teased.

"What? No," Kathleen said quickly. "Please forgive me for being so forward. It's just that I have read so much about you."

Kohrs laughed easily. "There is nothing to

79

forgive. I was making joke with you. But one should not always believe everything one reads," Kohrs said. "You ask your friend about that. There have been so many . . . what are they called . . . dime novels . . . written about him that I'm sure every young boy in America knows about him. Or thinks they know about him."

Falcon laughed and nodded. "This is true," he said.

"Something in here I wish to show you later," Kohrs said, patting a satchel.

"All right," Falcon answered. "Oh, by the way, I bring greetings to you from an old friend. Captain Sean MacTavish sends his regards."

"Sean MacTavish you met? He is a good man," Kohrs said. "A very good man. Together we sailed when I was much younger."

"Yes, he told me some of the stories," Falcon said. "Including one about the girls of France."

To Falcon's surprise, he could almost see the blush in Kohrs's face.

"Please, do not speak of such embarrassment in front of the young *fraulein*."

"Don't worry, Conrad," Falcon said. "The story will never be repeated."

"Sean is a good man," Kohrs said. "But

he talks too much, I think."

"Won't you join us?" Falcon offered.

"Danke," Kohrs replied, sitting in the proffered chair. "I won't stay long. I know that with your lady friend you will want to dance," Kohrs said. "But there is something I wish to tell you."

"You are welcome to visit for as long as you like."

"Today for the meeting, you were there?" Kohrs asked.

"I was there for some of it," Falcon answered. He smiled. "Though I confess I left for most of the afternoon."

"Did you hear, in the talking today, when the man from the meatpacking place says that he cannot pay so much for the cows because they do not weigh enough?"

Falcon nodded. "Yes, I was there when he said that. And as much as I hate to admit it, he has a point. You and I both know, Conrad, that sometimes, when the picking is sparse, the longhorns tend to get a little stringy," he said.

"Yes," Kohrs said. "But I have a plan to stop that."

Falcon chuckled. "How are you going to stop a cow from getting stringy if he has to scratch up ten acres just to get fed?"

"First, I have something I want you to

81

see," Kohrs said.

"In the satchel?" Falcon asked.

"No, that is later. What I want you to see now, you cannot put in a satchel." He held his hand up and called one of the waiters over.

"Paul, the special beef, bring to this table now," he said. "And in two plates, one for the lady."

"Yes, sir, Mr. Kohrs."

"I have a steak I want you to eat," Kohrs said, explaining his order to Falcon.

"Thank you, Mr. Kohrs, but I've eaten," Falcon said, patting his stomach. "We both have."

"This is not for dinner to eat," Kohrs said. "This is for you to taste. You and the lady," he said, looking across the table toward Kathleen. "I want to be certain that you *verstehen,* you . . . understand," he said, searching for the English word. "Please, for me, I wish you to do this."

"All right," Falcon said, not quite sure where Kohrs was going with this.

A moment later the waiter returned carrying a tray, protected by a silver cover. Lifting the cover revealed two plates. On each of the two plates was a small but very thickly cut steak. Each of the steaks bore the striping of having been grilled. And even though

Falcon had already eaten, the aroma of the steaks was irresistible.

But it was Kathleen who put the moment in words.

"Oh, my!" she said. "Has there ever been a more divine aroma."

"The aroma, it is nothing," Kohrs said. "It is the taste you must experience."

Falcon carved off a piece of the steak and put it in his mouth. The steak was juicy, and delicious. But what was most noticeable was how tender it was. Falcon had never eaten a piece of meat this tender.

"Oh, how heavenly!" Kathleen said, smacking her lips in delight. "You must tell me what the cook did to make this steak taste so delicious."

"Nothing special did the cook do," Kohrs replied. "We cook this steak as we cook any steak," Kohrs said.

Falcon shook his head. "No, it isn't like any steak. It's like no steak I've ever tasted before."

Kohrs held up his finger and wagged it back and forth. "That it is like any other steak I did not say. I said it was cooked like any other steak. But this steak is from Hereford cow," Kohr said. "Hereford cows are much bigger than longhorn cows, and much better is the meat."

"I won't argue with you there."

"In Laramie, Wyoming, in one month, there will be many Hereford cows for sale, both bulls and cows. There will be many who are going to go there to buy some seed bulls and brood heifers so we can begin raising Herefords instead of longhorns," Kohr said. "We will change forever the cattle business."

"You say many of us. Who will that be?"

"I will be in Laramie when the sale begins. Also John Iliff, C.C. Slaughter, George Littlefield, Shanghai Pierce, Alexander Swan, Pierre Wibaux, Granville Stuart, and Dudley Snyder."

Falcon let out a low whistle. "The men you just named are responsible for almost half the cattle produced in this country. I can see why you expect to change the cattle business forever."

"I think you should be there too."

"I will admit that it does sound interesting," Falcon said.

"If we are to forever change the cattle business, you must be there," Kohrs said. "You are an important man. When others hear that you are raising Herefords, they will want to raise them as well."

Falcon shook his head. "Important? Come on, Conrad, you know better than that.

When people hear the word 'cattleman,' I'm not the first one they think of. Besides, with that list of names you just gave me, it would seem to me that you have this pretty well tied up."

"But your name *is* well known," Kohrs insisted. "And if they don't think cattle when they think your name, that is the more better. They will think that even one who does not have so many cows can raise Herefords."

"I have a question."

"What is the question?"

"Why are you trying to recruit so many people? Wouldn't it be better for you if you had the Herefords all to yourself?"

Kohrs shook his head. "No," he said. "If only I raise Herefords, then the meatpackers will pay me no more than they are paying for longhorn cattle. And if I refuse to sell, they will not mind because they will have other cattlemen from whom they can get their beef." Kohrs held up his finger. "But if all of us have Hereford cattle to sell, they will have to pay us what the cattle are worth. And because the cows are bigger, even the meatpackers will make more of a profit."

"I see your point."

"It is not just the men I have named who

are coming. From all over the West, cattlemen will come to buy cows. On that day, I believe, the little town of Laramie will have more money than any city in the West."

Falcon drummed his fingers on the table as he listened to Kohrs make his case.

"Mr. Kohrs, I can see why you are so successful," he said. "All right, you have talked me into it. I will go to Laramie to buy Herefords."

"*Gut, gut,* then there a beer I will buy for you," Kohrs said, smiling broadly over his success in recruiting Falcon. He reached down into his satchel and pulled out an envelope. "And now this is what I want you to see. Tonight, before to sleep you go, I want you to read."

"All right," Falcon said, taking the envelope. "I'll read it tonight."

"I must say," Kathleen said after Kohrs walked away from the table, "he is a very impressive man."

"Yes, and persuasive," Falcon said. He sighed. "I had no intention of going to Laramie, but he has talked me into it."

"Is it true, what I read about him? Does he really have a hundred thousand cows."

"I imagine he does," Falcon said.

"Then it was true."

"As far as you read. But let me tell you

about the real Conrad Kohrs," Falcon said.

"The real Conrad Kohrs? And who is the real Conrad Kohrs?"

"He has lived a life that most men can only dream about," Falcon began. "He was born in Germany, but at the age of fifteen he went to sea as a cabin boy, and for the next seventeen years led the life of a seaman, sailing all over the world."

"My, how exciting that all sounds," Kathleen said. "But how did he wind up in America?"

"He just got tired of the sea," Falcon said. "So he jumped ship in New York, where he did some work as a butcher, while also working occasionally for relatives in New York and Iowa. Then he began traveling around the country, selling sausages in New Orleans, running logs down the Mississippi, and working in a distillery. But in 1857 he became a United States citizen, followed by his trek to the West. If you ask him what he owed his good fortune to, he would say it was just luck. But anyone who knows him knows better. He is successful because of his intelligence, experience, and most of all his hard work."

"He sounds like quite a man," Kathleen said. She put her hand across the table and rested it on top of his hand. "But then, I have heard the same things about you."

"Impossible. You just met me today."

"It is true that I just met you today," Kathleen said. "But I've known about you for a long time."

"Please don't tell me you have read those awful dime novels," Falcon said with a groan.

Kathleen laughed. "I'm innocent," she said. "I've never read one."

"Well, I'm thankful for that," he said.

The music began playing, and Kathleen reached across the table to put her hand on Falcon's arm. "Aren't you going to invite me to dance?" she asked.

It was very warm in the hotel room, and Falcon lay on top of the bedcovers, reading the report that Kohrs had given him. It was written in longhand, but the penmanship was sharp and very legible, making it easy to read.

A New Breed of Cows

Only a few copies of this report are being prepared, and it should be circulated with the greatest of care.

A changeover to the Hereford breed is going to require a rather significant investment on the part of the participating cattlemen. It is anticipated that the bidding for the seed bulls and blooded heifers with which to start the new herds will be quite brisk. It is suggested that those who wish to bid have at their disposal at least fifteen thousand dollars.

This information should not be shared with the general public, for fear of making the cost of participation much higher.

Falcon had just finished reading the report, and he put it on the table beside the bed when he heard a light knock on the door. Not expecting anyone at this late hour, he reached up to his holster belt, which was looped across the headboard of the bed, then eased the pistol from its holster.

"Who's there?" he called.

As soon as he called out, he moved quickly to one side of the room in case someone on the other side of the door decided to shoot toward the sound of the voice.

"It's Kathleen," a woman's voice answered.

"Kathleen? Is something wrong?" Falcon asked. He stepped over to the door and unlocked it, then pulled it open while at the same time stepping back out of the way. A pie-shaped wedge of golden light spilled into the room from the kerosene lamps that lit the hallway. Kathleen stepped into the wedge of light. She didn't see Falcon, but Falcon could see her. She was wearing a silk nightgown that clung to her curves in a way that hid nothing of her charms. And since he had seen her earlier in the bath, he knew exactly what those charms were.

"Falcon?" she called in confusion. "Mr. MacCallister, are you here?"

"Yes," Falcon said quietly while remaining in the shadows alongside the door.

"Why are you hiding?"

"I'm not exactly hiding," Falcon replied. "I'm just being cautious."

Kathleen's laugh was low and throaty. "Why, Mr. MacCallister, are you afraid of me?"

"Why do you ask? Should I be afraid?" Falcon asked. He stepped out of the shadows.

"I would hope that you aren't afraid," Kathleen said. "After all, I'm just a woman." She punctuated her comment by thrusting her hip to one side and smiling up at him.

Kathleen had put on some perfume and Falcon could smell its scent: a touch of lilac, a hint of coriander and something else; a womanly musk that came not from the perfume, but from her own excitement.

"I couldn't sleep," Kathleen said. "I thought maybe, that is, if you couldn't sleep either, we might . . ." She paused for a moment, as if thinking of the right word, then, with a seductive smile said, "Visit."

"Do come in," Falcon invited.

Six

One week later, Johnny Purvis was sitting on the bunk when Sheriff Foster opened the door.

"Out of the cell," the sheriff ordered.

"What do you want?"

"I want you out of the cell," Foster said again.

Johnny stroked his scar nervously. "Look, I don't know what this is about, but I ain't even had a trial yet."

"You aren't getting a trial."

"What do you mean, I ain't gettin' a trial? Ever'one gets a trial."

"The woman whose room you broke into?" Foster said. "She never came by to file a complaint. Without her complaint and statement, we can't hold you."

Johnny smiled broadly, then grabbed his hat. "So what you're sayin' is, you're lettin' me go?"

"That's what I'm saying."

"Ha!" Johnny said. "I know'd you couldn't hold me. I told you, I wasn't doin' nothin' wrong. I was just in the wrong room."

"Yeah, so you said."

"Wait a minute. What you lettin' me go now for? It's about lunchtime, ain't it?"

"Yes."

"Yeah, I thought so. I'm hungry. Why don't you wait and let me go after lunch?"

"Huh-uh," Foster said, shaking his head. "You aren't the county's problem anymore," he said. "You want lunch, you're goin' to have to pay for it yourself."

"I ain't got enough money for lunch," Johnny said.

Foster sighed, then reached into his pocket and pulled out a quarter. "Here," he said, handing the coin to Johnny. "This'll get you a plate lunch down at Little Man Lambert's."

"That was a really good meal, Little Man," one of the diners at the café said as he stopped by the counter to pay for his dinner.

"Well, thank you, Mr. Ferrell," the restaurant owner replied.

Ferrell pulled out a roll of money and Little Man whistled.

"That's an awful lot of money to be flash-

93

ing around, isn't it?" he asked.

"I know," Ferrell said. "But it's payday for all my hands. Like as not you'll be getting a few of 'em in here tonight. That is, the ones that are still sober come supper time. Whenever they get paid, they like to spend their money in town."

"I'll get some of it," Little Man agreed. "But more'n likely, most of it will wind up with the girls over at the Turner Theater."

Ferrell laughed. "I don't doubt that," he said. "Well, you're only young once," he added. "I can't hold it against 'em."

Johnny was sitting at a table very near the counter, and he overheard the conversation between Ferrell and Little Man. Then, finishing his meal, he went up to the counter.

"Was your meal satisfactory, sir?"

"Yeah, it was fine," Johnny grunted, slapping the quarter down on the counter.

"We have cherry pie today," Little Man said.

"I ain't got no more money."

"Oh, the pie comes with the meal. You've already paid for it."

"No, thanks."

All the time Johnny was talking to Little Man, he was looking through the window, keeping an eye on Ferrell. He saw Ferrell walk across the street and step into the livery.

Little Man chuckled. "I don't know as I've ever seen anyone turn down a piece of cherry pie."

"I ain't got time for no more palaverin'," Johnny growled.

The smile left Little Man's face. "Then go on," he said. "Don't let me stop you."

Leaving the café, Johnny hurried down the street, crossed over to the other side, then went between two buildings in order to emerge in the alley. Moving quickly up the alley, he came up to the back end of the livery stable. The corral of the stable was enclosed by a fence, and Johnny climbed over the fence, then darted across the corral to the big, wide, double doors. He pushed them open just enough to get through, then closed them behind him.

It was dark in the stable, the only light being the irregular, glistening mote-filled bars of sun that speared through the cracks between the wide, unpainted boards. Johnny stood still for a moment until his eyes adjusted to the dark. Then he saw Ferrell standing at one of the stalls, feeding an apple to a horse. Seeing a pitchfork leaning against the wall, Johnny picked it up, then started toward Ferrell.

"I don't know why I put up with you," Ferrell was saying to his horse.

The horse whickered, and Ferrell patted it on the nose. He was so engrossed with his horse that he did not notice the man moving quietly through the shadows behind him.

Johnny raised the pitchfork.

Ferrell heard, or sensed something behind him. Turning, he didn't even have time to cry out before Johnny plunged the pitchfork into his chest.

Ferrell made a gurgling noise and blood oozed from his mouth as he went down. Johnny reached over and took the wad of money from him, even as Ferrell's eyes were growing opaque. Sticking the money into his pocket, he left the livery stable by the same way he had entered, out the back doors, across the corral past the boarded horses, then over the fence and back down the alley.

A train was pulling into the station just as he reached the depot. Johnny barely had time enough to by a ticket to Boise, Idaho Territory, before the train pulled out. As the train left, Johnny looked up the street toward the livery stable. He saw a dozen or more people gathered around the front, and he saw Sheriff Foster coming quickly to the scene.

Johnny smiled. Ferrell's body had been discovered, but he was safely on the train, leaving town. He felt a tremendous sense of elation, almost as if he were drunk. It wasn't until then that he took the time to count his money. It was two hundred and forty dollars.

Gabe Harland and Pete Ward reached the little town of Carriso at about ten o'clock in the evening. Carriso was divided into two sections, the American section and the Mexican section. The two sections of town were separated by the Union Pacific Railroad and though they were within walking distance of each other, so little interchange existed between the two elements that it could have been two different towns.

The American section, on the north side of the tracks, had false-fronted buildings made of lumber flanking straight, well-defined streets. The saloon served beer and American whiskey, and the cooking smells from the residential area were of fried pork chops or chicken. Potatoes and biscuits were the staple.

The Mexican section on the south side was made up of adobe structures, and the smells from here were spicy, with beans and tortillas being the staple. The streets were crooked and irregular, and the cantina served tequila.

Tired and frustrated over a bank robbery that netted very little, Gabe and Pete decided there would be less chance of anyone recognizing them if they stayed on the Mexican side. Gabe could speak the lingo, but Pete couldn't, which put him at a disadvantage.

There were two men standing in front of the cantina. Both were wearing large sombreros, and one was wearing a serape.

"Por que ha venido aquí un gringo?" the Mexican with the serape asked.

The other shrugged. *"No se. Tal vez estan perdidos."*

"We are not lost," Gabe answered in English. "And we came here to get a bottle of tequila and a whore."

"The gringos don't have *putas?*" the one with the serape asked.

"Yes, but all American whores are ugly," Gabe said.

The two Mexicans laughed.

"Enjoy your tequila and your *puta,* señor."

Nodding, Gabe and Pete pushed through the hanging beads, causing them to clack loudly as the two men went inside.

"*Sí, señor?*" the bartender asked.

"Tequila," Gabe said. "Two bottles."

"Pick out a whore," Gabe said to Pete.

"I heard what you said to them Mexes out front," Pete said. "But to tell the truth, I don't like Mexican whores as much as I like American whores."

"It don't matter, you're gettin' 'em as much for the bed as for anything else," Gabe said.

Gabe woke up the next morning with a ravenous hunger and a raging need to urinate. The *puta* was still asleep beside him. She had the bedcover askew, exposing one enormous, pillow-sized, heavily blue-veined breast. One fat leg dangled over the edge of the bed. She was snoring loudly and a bit of spittle drooled from her vibrating lips. She didn't wake up when Gabe crawled over her to get out of bed and get dressed.

There was an outhouse just behind the cantina, no more than twenty feet from the door of this very room, but Gabe made no attempt to go outside. Instead, he urinated against the wall.

"Pete!" he called as he stood there, relieving himself. "Pete, are you still in there?"

Pete had gone with the *puta* into the room next door. Gabe heard someone walking up

99

the hall; then Pete appeared in the doorway. Pete was wearing his boots and a hat, but nothing more. He joined Gabe, urinating on the wall.

"What are we doin' here, Gabe?" Pete asked.

Gabe chuckled. "Well, I'm takin' a pee," he said. "And it's a good thing you're naked, 'cause you're takin' a pee too."

"I know that," Pete said. "What I want to know is, why did we come to this town? There's lots of Mex towns we could'a gone to."

"Yeah, but Eddie Jordan lives in this town. You remember Eddie Jordan, don't you?"

"Yeah, I remember Eddie Jordan. What are you lookin' for him for?"

Gabe shook himself, then turned away from the wall. "We need some money, don't we?"

"Yeah, I reckon we do."

"Well, if there's somethin' goin' on anywhere, Eddie's the one who will know about it."

"You mean like another robbery?"

"Yeah," Gabe said. "Only this time, maybe we can pick us a bank that has more than sixty-five dollars in it."

"Are we goin' over into the American side to look for him?"

"Nah, we ain't. She is," Gabe said, nodding toward the sleeping whore. "Get dressed. I'll send her after Eddie while we have breakfast."

"All right," Pete said.

"*Puta. Puta.* Wake up," Gabe called.

The woman in the bed groaned irritably and turned over.

"*Puta.* Wake up, *puta.*"

"*Qué quiere usted, señor?*"

"What do I want? I want you to go find someone for me. That's what I want."

"*Qué?*"

"*Quiero que usted* go *conseguir alguien para mí,*" Gabe said, repeating the request mostly in Spanish this time.

Gabe and Pete were halfway through their breakfast when Gabe's whore came into the café followed by a tall, gangly American. The expression on the American's face was one of curiosity, since it was obvious he had no idea as to why she had come north of the tracks to summon him.

"He is there, señor," the whore said, pointing toward Gabe and Pete.

When Eddie saw the two men, he smiled, then came over to join them, taking a chair from a nearby table.

"Well, I'll be damn," Eddie said. Without

being invited, he picked up a tortilla, rolled it around some beans, then took a bite. "If it ain't Gabe Harland and Pete Ward. What are you two doing here?"

"Ever'one has to be somewhere," Gabe answered.

Eddie chuckled. "Well, you got that right," he said. "But as long as you're going to be in Carriso, what are you doin' on the Mexican side?"

"Maybe you didn't hear about it," Gabe said. "But me'n Pete robbed a bank down in Erastus."

"Really? Then I'll ask the question again. If you've got all that money, what the hell are you doing in a flyspeck like Carriso?"

"We didn't get all that much money," Gabe said.

"Oh? How much did you get?"

"Sixty-five dollars," Pete said, mumbling around a burrito. His words were so mumbled as to be unintelligible.

"How much?" Eddie asked.

"Sixty-five dollars," Pete said. Again, he mumbled the words so quietly that Eddie couldn't hear them.

"I still didn't hear."

"We got sixty-five dollars," Gabe said, clearly and distinctly.

Eddie looked at the two men for a moment; then he burst out into loud laughter, spraying bits of chewed food onto the table.

"Sixty-five dollars?" he said, wiping his mouth with the back of his hand. "You robbed a bank, and all you got was sixty-five dollars?"

"That's all the money they had in the damn thing," Gabe said with disgust. He sighed. "But the point is, we did rob the bank, and it don't make no difference how much was took, the law will be after us just the same. So, we figured we'd better stay on this side of town."

Eddie nodded, though he was still fighting the giggles.

"Well, I'm glad you are finding it so damn funny," Gabe said.

"I'm sorry," Eddie said. "I know it ain't funny to you. I mean you take just as big a chance robbing a bank for sixty-five dollars as you do for ten thousand dollars."

"Yeah," Gabe said. He sighed. "But what's done is done. And we still need money."

"Look, I know I owe you twenty dollars," Eddie said. He reached into his pocket and pulled out a twenty-dollar gold piece. "And I would'a give it to you a long time ago, but I kind'a lost track of where you was."

"I didn't come here to collect the twenty dollars," Gabe said, though even as he denied it, he was pocketing the coin. "What I come here for was to see if you had any ideas."

"Ideas about what?" Eddie said.

Gabe shook his head. "Come on, Eddie, don't make me spell it out for you. Because if I do spell it out, someone might hear it. Someone that we don't want to hear what we are talkin' about."

"What are we talkin' about?" Eddie asked.

Gabe sighed. "Don't play games with me, Eddie. I know that you always know what's goin' on. And whatever it is, I want in on it."

Eddie drummed his fingers on the table for a moment; then he nodded.

"All right, I do know about something that's going on. And from what I hear, it's going to be a lot of money."

"Who? When? Where?"

Eddie shook his head. "No," he said. "I can't tell you anything yet. Not until I find out if it's all right to bring you two in."

"What do you mean, find out as if it's all right? You know us. Can't you tell whoever it is about us?"

"Stay here for a few days," Eddie said.

"For how long?"

"Until I find out if it's all right."

"But how long will that be?"

Eddie chuckled. "Hell, Gabe, you got food, liquor, and whores. What else do you need?" he asked.

"You say it's a lot of money?" Gabe asked.

Eddie nodded. "A lot of money," he said.

Gabe looked across the table at Pete, who had not stopped eating from the moment they sat down to breakfast.

"What do you think, Pete? Shall we wait?"

Pete nodded, but did not verbalize his response.

"All right," Gabe said. "We'll wait."

"You won't be sorry," Eddie said as he left.

SEVEN

Established by a group of gold prospectors on November 22, 1858, and named after James Denver, the governor of Kansas Territory at the time, Denver had grown in just one generation to be the second-largest city in the West. The city of Denver had more people than the territories of the Dakotas, Wyoming, Arizona, and New Mexico combined.

Gilly Cardis had never been in a city so large. His first sight was of the railroad depot itself. He stepped down, not onto a wooden platform from a single train stopped next to a small depot as he was used to, but onto a cement walk that separated the train he was on from another train next to it.

"Make way, make way!" someone shouted, and Cardis had to step aside quickly to avoid being run down by someone pushing a baggage cart.

Cardis happened to glance up then and

saw that, though he was off the train, he wasn't outside. Instead, he was under a high overhead roof, made of corrugated tin and supported by a network of pillars and cables. He saw also that there were actually several trains under this roof. One train was leaving, while another train was backing into the station. And his train and the next train over were but two of several trains that were in the station.

He could hear trains backing in and pulling out, the sound of puffing steam engines echoing back from the overhead roof. Following the crowd of people who left the train, Cardis walked into the depot itself. The building was huge, bigger than any building Cardis had ever seen in his life. The floor was of marble, and stretched over the top of the depot was a large dome, which acted as an amplifier for the hundreds of conversations that echoed back. He could also hear, and feel, the rumbling movement of the heavy trains as they rolled in and out of the rail yard.

Looking back toward the door through which he had just passed, he saw a sign that read:

TO TRAINS

On the opposite wall, all the way across the floor, beyond the scores of long wooden benches upon which passengers were sitting as they awaited the departure of their trains, was another sign. This one read:

TO STREET

On one wall was a huge clock, flanked on either side by gigantic blackboards upon which updated information was imparted to the passengers. One of the blackboards listed destinations, track numbers, and times of departure. The other blackboard listed points of origin, track numbers, and times of arrival.

Cardis saw cities listed that he had never visited, but only heard about: San Francisco, St. Louis, Memphis, Chicago, New York, Boston, Philadelphia.

The depot was filled with people, and everyone seemed to be in a hurry. He tried to stop a couple of people to ask them a question, but they moved on without responding. Then he saw two men who didn't seem to be in as big a hurry as everyone else, but were standing in the middle of the floor talking to each other. He walked up to them.

"Can you tell me whereat I can find me a

man who calls hisself MacCallister? Falcon MacCallister?"

"No, I don't think so," one of the men answered.

"How come you don't know? I'm told he lives near Denver."

One of the men laughed. "Mister, one hundred thousand people live in Denver. Do you expect us to know every one?"

"One hundred thousand?" Cardis replied, shocked by the number.

"It may be larger," the other man suggested.

Shaking his head, Cardis walked away from the two. That was when he noticed the long counter, topped by a frosted-glass wall. The glass wall was interrupted every few feet by windows, and behind each window was a ticket agent. He walked up to one of the windows.

"Yes, sir," the ticket agent greeted. "Where would you like to go?"

"I ain't a' goin' nowhere, I just got here," Cardis said. "I was just a' wonderin' if you could tell me whereat a fella by the name of Falcon MacCallister might live."

The ticket agent shook his head. "I'm sorry," he said. "I don't think I can help you." Looking over Cardis's shoulder, the ticket agent called out to a woman who was standing behind him. "Next."

"Well, have you got 'ny idea —" Cardis started, but the ticket agent interrupted him.

"Excuse me, sir, but I do have a customer and as there are train schedules to keep, I can't keep her waiting."

Cardis walked away, then headed for the door under the sign that said TO STREET.

The street in front of the depot was so filled with hacks, carriages, buggies, buckboards, and freight wagons that it was difficult for Cardis to get to the other side.

Cardis wandered around the city for the rest of the day, marveling at the crowds of people and size of all the buildings. When it grew dark, he realized that he was hungry, so he walked around until he found a restaurant. A waiter escorted him to an empty table, then gave him a menu.

"I'll give you a moment to make up your mind," he said.

Cardis opened the menu, then gasped in surprise at the cost of everything. He had thought that he would have enough money to spend a few days in Denver, at least until he found MacCallister. But if the cost of meals in this restaurant was any indication, he was going to have to make up his mind whether he wanted to eat or sleep warm.

For now, he decided that he would eat.

But since most of the thirty-one dollars he had stolen was gone, he was going to have to make some kind of arrangements. Normally, he wouldn't even think twice about staying in a hotel. But now he would find a livery somewhere. Most of the time he could sleep in the warm straw in a livery stable for free. Sometimes it would cost him a nickel or maybe even a dime, but never more than that.

Cardis ordered fried chicken and ate heartily, breaking the bones and sucking out the marrow. Then he used a piece of bread to sop up everything from the plate. When he was finished, he stepped outside. It was dark and foggy and Cardis, who wasn't wearing a coat, was surprised by how cold it was. Three days ago he had been fighting the desert heat. Now he was so cold that he couldn't stop shivering, and he stuck his hands down in his pockets as he walked off into the night.

A hansom cab rolled by, the horses' hooves clattering loudly on the cobblestone street. The cab was dark brown with yellow trim and yellow wheels. The seats were cushioned leather, and the passenger sitting in the back was wearing a suit, overcoat, and top hat. He had the arrogant look of someone who was not only used to such luxury, but accepted it as his due.

"Stop here, Clarence," the man called, and the cab stopped about half a block in front of Cardis. Cardis stepped back into the shadows.

"You sure you want to stop here, Mr. Brooks?" the driver, Clarence, said. "I can take you right to your house with no problem."

"No, you'd have to go all the way down to the bottom of the hill, around the block, then back up again," Brooks said. "I can just cut through the alley."

"Yes, sir, if you say so."

Brooks got out and stepped up to the front of the cab, then paid the driver.

"Your team was stepping out quite lively tonight, Clarence. I enjoyed the ride."

"Thank you, sir," Clarence replied. Clarence clucked at his team, then snapped the reins. They started up again, and the cab disappeared quickly into the fog bank.

Although Cardis could no longer see the cab, he could hear it as it continued down the street. He could also see the golden bubbles of light that marked each corner of the avenue. These were the streetlamps, gleaming yellow, though with a light so diffused by the mist that they provided little in the way of illumination.

Staying well back, Cardis followed Brooks for about half a block until he turned up an alley that had no lights at all. Within a moment, Brooks was swallowed up in the night and the fog.

Cardis darted up a side street that ran parallel with the alley, then he came to a cross-alley. He ran down the cross-alley, then leaned against the cold, damp, brick wall, breathing hard as he waited for Brooks to arrive. The fog was so thick that he couldn't see ten feet in front of him. But he could hear Brooks's footsteps echoing hollowly in the darkness.

The footsteps came closer and closer until Brooks passed to within the little ten-foot bubble of visibility. Cardis waited for just a second, then, with his pistol drawn, he suddenly jumped out in front of him.

"No!" Brooks gasped, seeing the gun in Cardis's hand. "No!"

Cardis pulled the trigger. The gunshot sounded exceptionally loud to him, echoing back and forth from the walls of the buildings that flanked the alley. Even before the last echo died, several dogs within the neighborhood began barking.

"What was that?" a frightened voice called from somewhere in the darkness.

"A shot! I heard a shot!" another answered.

From somewhere far off, Cardis could hear the two-tone bleat of a policeman's whistle, but because he felt shielded by the night and the fog, he was able to reach leisurely into Brooks's pocket and take out his billfold. Opening the billfold, he smiled broadly when he saw that it was fat with banknotes. He took the money, then dropped the billfold onto Brooks's body.

By now he could hear footsteps running up the street, and a second police whistle joined the first. But the footsteps were still on the street, not in the alley, so Cardis was undisturbed by all the commotion that was going on around him.

Moving quickly back up the cross-alley, Cardis came back out onto the street. Then, ahead, he saw a marquee out over the sidewalk. The sign on the marquee read: ALPINE HOTEL.

Cardis went inside. It had been a long time since he'd actually stayed in a hotel. But he had enough money now to do so, so he stepped up to the desk. There was no one there, so he waited.

A man came into the hotel lobby, wearing a domed hat and a long blue coat with a double row of brass buttons. Cardis had never seen a uniformed policeman before, and for a moment he was startled, because the uniform reminded him a lot of the uniforms the guards wore back in the Yuma prison. Seeing Cardis standing calmly by the desk, the policeman spoke to him.

"I'm Officer Williams. Has anyone come running in here in the last few minutes?"

Cardis shook his head. "No, I ain't seen no one. Why? What happened?"

"There was a murder very close to here," the policeman said.

"Did the murderer get away?" Cardis asked.

"Let's just say that we haven't found him yet," the policeman said. "But we will. In the meantime, as dark and foggy as it is outside, and with a murderer on the loose, I'd suggest that you stay inside for the night."

"Yeah, I will," Cardis said.

Shortly after the policeman left, the desk clerk appeared.

"I'm sorry, sir, I was, uh, temporarily detained," the desk clerk said. "Have you been here long?"

"Yes."

"Why didn't you ring the bell?"

"What bell? I don't see no bell."

The clerk pointed to a small half-round

object on the desk, from which a button protruded. He slapped the button with the palm of his hand, and the bell rang.

"I'll be damn," Cardis said, examining the little bell. "I sure ain't never seen nothin' like that."

"Would you like a room?"

"Yeah."

The clerk turned the registration book around for Cardis to fill out.

"Am I right? Was a policeman just in here?" the clerk asked.

"Yeah. He just left."

"What did he want?"

"There was a murder near here," Cardis said as he finished filling out the book. "He said we should stay inside."

"He needn't worry. I intend to do just that." The clerk took a key from a board and handed it to Cardis. "You are in room twenty-four, second floor, all the way to the back," the clerk said.

Cardis paid no attention to the dozen or so roaches that started running across the floor when he lit the lantern. It also didn't bother him that the linen on the iron-stead bed was dirty, and had probably not been changed for several weeks. A fading brown chest of drawers was set against a wall from

116

which hung strips of loose wallpaper. A porcelain basin and a pitcher of water was on the chest of drawers, alongside a chamber pot that reeked of urine. The window shade was badly torn, and the windowpane was cracked.

Cardis took the chamber pot down and used it, then he opened the window and poured the urine out. He stood at the window for a moment, but because of the fog and darkness, couldn't see anything.

Then, turning away from the window, he sat on the bed and began counting the money he had taken from Brooks. The total came to fifty-six dollars. That should keep him in town long enough to find MacCallister.

EIGHT

Jamie's Ridge, named after Falcon's father, Jamie Ian MacCallister, sat at the north end of MacCallister Valley. Stretching across the valley, it stood like a closed door against the cold winds of winter. It didn't keep out all the cold, of course, but its effect was noticeable. Often, while neighboring counties would get two or three feet of snow, the snow falling in MacCallister Valley would be calculated in inches. And during the great "Winter Freeze Out" of a few years ago, when hundreds of thousands of head of cattle died all over the West, the cattle in MacCallister Valley fared surprisingly well.

Falcon rode up to the crest of Jamie's Ridge, then dismounted and, as Diablo cropped grass, Falcon sat on a large, flat rock and looked out over the valley. The setting sun caught the stream that ran through the middle of the valley, turning it molten gold. And indeed, the stream was gold as far as the valley was concerned because its inexhaustible supply of water was fully as valuable to the business of raising cattle as were the gently rolling grasslands.

Anytime Falcon was home, particularly if he wanted to think about something, he would come here. In fact, he could almost believe that the rock he was sitting on was flat because he had so often sat on it. Right now, he wanted to think about what he and Kohrs had discussed. Did he really want to replace his longhorns with Herefords?

It wasn't entirely a business decision that caused him to pause and think. He knew that Kohrs was right about the value of Herefords, and the role they would play in the future of the cattle industry. Herefords would make more money.

But money was not a problem with Falcon. He had mineral rights to gold and silver mines; in fact, the Arizona silver mine that he had recently bought from Doc Holliday was already paying off handsomely.

But he liked the longhorns. He admired their tenacity and their ability to find something to eat when the deer and the antelope could not. That was good for someone like him. He wasn't exactly a "stay at home" rancher. Ever since his father and wife had been killed by renegade Indians,

Falcon MacCallister had been a man on the move. He did not see that changing anytime soon.

He also liked the continuity of the longhorns. These had been the cattle of his father, and by looking at them, he could almost project himself back to a happier time, when his father and his wife were both alive, and he was a serious rancher.

On the other hand, he felt that he owed an obligation to the valley that his father had been so instrumental in settling and building. And if his obligation was to introduce a breed of cattle that would take them into the future, then he should do so. The days of the longhorn were numbered, and anyone who did not make the transition into the new breed would be left behind.

Falcon reached down and pulled up a stem of grass, then put the sweet root into his mouth and sucked on it.

"Wait a minute," he said aloud. "Diablo, who says that I have to get rid of my longhorns? Why can't I raise both breeds?"

Falcon knew that talking to Diablo was little more than talking to himself, but sometimes it was effective in helping him think things out. Smiling, he stood up, and walked back over to Diablo. Patting his horse on the neck, he spoke into his ear.

"Thanks," he said. "I just needed to talk to someone who could give me a little advice, and you have been very helpful."

He remounted, then started back toward the house, his mind made up.

Falcon packed his bags for the trip, then rode into town to buy a ticket and make arrangements to take his horse with him.

It was very dark by the time the train pulled into Laramie, Wyoming, but the station platform was so brightly lit by nearly a dozen gas lamps that it shined like a golden bubble. Falcon got off the train, then walked up to the stock car to wait for Diablo to be offloaded.

"Staying in town long?" the stationmaster asked.

"Staying through the auction," Falcon replied.

The stationmaster chuckled. "I thought maybe you were. We've got a lot of people in town right now. You lookin' for a place to stay? Because if you need a place, my sister-in-law rents a room in her house. Meals come with it, and I can attest to the fact that she's a good cook."

"Your sister-in-law?"

"Yes, she's a widow woman now. She was married to my brother."

"I don't know," Falcon said. "It probably wouldn't work out for your sister-in-law. I like to stay out late. I wouldn't want to disturb her when I come in."

"No problem. The back bedroom you would be using has its own door."

Falcon had planned to get a room in the hotel but, for some reason, he found the idea of staying in a private home strangely appealing.

"Does she have a place to put up my horse?"

"She has a barn out back," the station-master said. "Clean straw in the stall, fresh hay."

"Where is this place?"

"That's it, right across the street," the stationmaster said, pointing to a small, single-story wood-frame house. "Her name is Frances Martin. My name's Cody Martin. Tell her that I sent you. That way, she'll know you aren't dangerous."

"How do you know I'm not dangerous, Cody?" Falcon asked.

"Oh, you're a dangerous man, Falcon MacCallister," Cody said. "But you're only dangerous to those folks who cross you the wrong way."

"You know who I am?"

"Yes, sir, I know'd who you was the moment you stepped down from the train. I seen you in action once. Quick as thought, you were. But you was in the right, and the other fella was in the wrong. No, sir, you ain't no danger to my sister-in-law. Fact is, I'd feel comforted by you stayin' there."

Falcon nodded. "I appreciate your confidence in me," he said.

Falcon threw his saddle onto Diablo's back, but he didn't cinch it down. Instead, he walked across the street, leading his horse. Tying him off at the hitching post in front, Falcon walked up to the house and knocked on the front door.

A young boy answered the door. Falcon guessed that he was about fourteen.

"Yes, sir?" the boy said.

"I was told by the stationmaster that I could rent a room here," Falcon said.

The boy turned. "Mom!" he shouted.

"Don't shout so, Gordon, it's quite rude," a woman's voice said from within the house.

The stationmaster had said that his sister-in-law was a widow and, because of that, Falcon had a preconceived notion of what she might look like. The woman who answered her son's call wasn't at all what he had expected. She was probably in her early forties, but her skin had the peaches-and-cream complexion of someone much younger. Her high cheekbones, green eyes, and light brown hair were combined in just the exact proportion to make her an exceptionally pretty woman. Her beauty was what Falcon would describe as classic, rather than the seductive, almost hard-edged look that was common to so many of the younger women he encountered.

"Yes?" she said.

"Good evening, Mrs. Martin. As I told the boy, the stationmaster said I might be able to get a room here during my stay. He said to tell you that Cody Martin sent me."

The woman smiled, then opened the door. "Yes, that would be my brother-in-law. Please come in," she invited.

Falcon picked up his grip and went inside.

"The charge for the room and meals will be two dollars per night, payable each day in advance," Mrs. Martin said. "I do not allow liquor in my house, so if you intend to drink you must go elsewhere to do so."

"Fair enough," Falcon said. "I'm told you have a room that has a private entrance? I wouldn't want to disturb the house by coming in late."

"Yes, there is a private entrance."

"I'll take the room," Falcon said. He gave her a ten-dollar bill. "I'll pay for five days in advance," he said.

"You don't have to pay that far in advance," Mrs. Martin said.

"I know, but I prefer to, if you don't mind."

"No, of course I don't mind, Mister . . . I'm sorry, I don't believe you told me your name."

"MacCallister. Falcon MacCallister."

"Falcon MacCallister?" the boy said loudly. "Are you really Falcon MacCallister?"

Falcon nodded. "That's really my name," he said.

"Wow!"

Mrs. Martin looked puzzled. "I'm sorry," she said. "Is this a name I should recognize?"

Falcon shook his head. "No, ma'am, there's no reason at all you should recognize the name."

"Mom, he is just the most famous gunfighter there is, that's all," Gordon said, awestruck by his proximity to Falcon.

"Gunfighter?" she said.

"Don't worry, Mom," Gordon said quickly, seeing that she was beginning to have second thoughts about renting to him. "He only kills bad men."

"I see," she said. "Well, I suppose I should be comforted by the fact that you kill only . . . bad . . . men."

Falcon sighed and reached for his luggage. "I'm sorry," he said. "Perhaps I should stay at the hotel. I've no wish to make you uncomfortable."

"Mom!" Gordon said, obviously disturbed that Falcon was going to go somewhere else.

"Don't be silly. Of course you are welcome. If my brother-in-law sent you, I'm sure it will be all right. Besides, you won't be able to get a room at the hotel anyway. Apparently, there is some auction about to take place and a lot of people are in town for that."

"Yes," Falcon said. "I am here for the auction as well."

"I don't understand. Why would a gunfighter be interested in an auction?"

Falcon laughed out loud. "I'm not what you would call a full-time gunfighter," he said.

"I'm sorry," Mrs. Martin said. "That was quite rude of me."

"No apology needed. If you don't mind, I'll put my horse in the back."

"I'll do it," Gordon said excitedly.

"Well, thank you," Falcon said. He gave Gordon a quarter.

"Wow! Thanks!" Gordon said, hurrying to tend to the horse.

"It's past time for supper," Mrs. Martin said. "But if you are hungry, I could fix you something."

"Thank you, but that's not necessary," Falcon said. "If you'll just show me to the room, I'll be fine."

NINE

After getting settled in his room, Falcon let himself out the back door and walked down the street to find a saloon. It was easy to find, because of all the golden patches of light that spilled through the windows and doors of the buildings. The brightest patch lay in the street in front of a building that was identified as the Gold Strike. Falcon pushed through the swinging doors and went inside.

The piano player was taking a break, sitting with his back to his instrument and drinking a whiskey as he looked out over the customers.

Falcon stepped up to the bar.

"What can I get you, friend?" the bartender asked, moving toward him.

"A beer," Falcon said.

With a nod, the bartender drew the beer, then handed the glass to him. A full head was on top of the glass.

Falcon blew off much of the foam, then, as was his habit when visiting a saloon for the first time, he turned to peruse the room. At one of the tables, a lively card game was in progress. The table was crowded with brightly colored poker chips and empty beer mugs. There were two brass spittoons within spitting distance of the players, but despite their presence, the floor around the table was riddled with expectorated tobacco quids and chewed cigar butts.

One of the players, shaking his head in disgust, pushed the chair back and stood up. "That's it for me, boys," he said. "The cards wasn't comin' my way tonight. I ain't drawed a winnin' hand in a coon's age."

One of the players looked over toward the bar and, seeing that Falcon was watching them, called out to him.

"Mister, you've been watchin' our game like you might be interested in playing. Would you care to join us?"

Falcon tossed the rest of his drink down, then wiped the back of his hand across his mouth.

"Thanks for the invite," he said. "I believe I will join you, if you don't mind."

The person who invited Falcon stood and extended his hand. "The name's Clyde

Puckett," he said. "I work at the rolling mill."

"The rolling mill?"

"Don't tell me you didn't see the rolling mill," Clyde said. "It's just the biggest building in the entire Wyoming Territory is all. We make railroad tracks."

"You evidently arrived on this evening's train," one of the other players said. "Had you arrived in the daytime, you would have been aware of its presence, not only by its size, but by the noxious smoke it spreads across our community."

"That noxious smoke provides employment for two hundred families," Clyde said defensively.

"I'm not complaining, just commenting."

"Tell him the rules, Clyde," one of the other players said. He was the player with the most chips.

"Here's the rules," Clyde explained. "What you take out of your pocket and put in front of you is all the money you can play with. And you can't go back for more."

"And you can't put any more in front of you than the most any of us have," one of the other men said. "We've got a lot of rich folks in town now, what with this cattle auction that's coming up, and we don't aim to let anyone come in here and start buying the pot by betting more than anyone can match."

"Sounds reasonable enough to me," Falcon said.

"And just so you know who to look out for, Mr. Bill Nye here has been the winner so far tonight," one of the other players said.

"I must confess to *a bene placeto* with the cards," Nye said.

"As you no doubt gather from his Latin, Mr. Nye is a lawyer, and everybody knows what a foul profession lawyers be."

The others around the table, including Nye, laughed.

"Listen to who's talking. I ask you, gentlemen, in all sincerity, can you trust a representative of the press? Mr. Hayford here" — Nye pointed to the person who had identified him as a lawyer — "is publisher of *The Sentinel,* our newspaper."

"At least he doesn't send messages in code," Clyde said. "What did you say? A benny pleaseto or something like that?"

"My dear boy," Nye said. "And to whom would I be sending secret messages? *A bene placeto* is merely a Latin phrase meaning I have been well pleased with the cards."

"Yeah, well, don't use no more of that. It's like you're cheatin' or something."

"Fortunately for you, Clyde, I also believe

131

in *absit iniuria verbis.*" Nye held up his finger. "And before you fly off the handle, that means that I take no insult from your words."

"Mr. Nye is also the postmaster," Hayford said.

"Former postmaster, my good man, former postmaster," Nye said. "On October first of last year, I sent a letter to the President of the United States tendering my resignation. Perhaps you would like to hear it."

"I would love to hear it," Hayford said. His broad smile told Falcon that he had heard it before and had set this up just for Falcon's benefit.

"Hey, fellas," someone in the saloon shouted. "Mr. Nye is going to resign as postmaster again."

"I've got to hear that," someone else said, and nearly everyone in the bar, men and women, gathered around the table to listen.

Nye, who was very aware that he was center of attention, made a big show of removing a folded piece of paper from his inside jacket pocket. He slid his glasses up the bridge of his nose, cleared his throat, then flattened the paper and looked around at his audience before he began to read.

"From the Postmaster, Laramie City,

Wyoming Territory, to the President of the United States," he read in a loud, stentorian voice.

"Sir: I beg leave at this time to officially tender my resignation as postmaster at this place, and in due form to deliver the great seal and the key to the front door of the office. The safe combination is set on the numbers 22,66,99, though I do not remember at this moment which comes first, or how many times you revolve the knob, or which direction you should turn it first in order to make it operate.

"There is some mining stock in my private drawer in the safe, which I have not yet removed. This stock you may have, if you desire it. It is a luxury, but you may have it. I have decided to keep a horse instead of this mining stock. The horse may not be so pretty, but it will cost less to keep him.

"You will find the postal cards that have not been used under the distributing table, and the coal down in the cellar. If the stove draws too hard, close the damper in the pipe and shut the general delivery window.

"Mr. President, as an official of this Government I now retire. My term of office would not expire until 1886. I must, therefore, beg pardon for my eccentricity in resigning. It would be best, perhaps, to keep the heartbreaking news of my resignation from the ears of European powers until the dangers of a financial panic are fully past. Then hurl it broadcast with a sickening thud.

"Yours sincerely, Bill Nye."

Nye's reading of his letter was met with laughter and applause, and he made a great show of bowing to his audience.

"Friend, I apologize for the interruption, and hope you will forgive us," Hayford said to Falcon. "But if you know anything about lawyers, you know what hams they are."

"Quit wasting the man's time with bogus apologies," Nye said. He looked at Falcon. "Do you have any questions about the rules of the game?"

"I take it I can match the funds of the person with the highest amount of money?" Falcon said.

"You can indeed, sir," Nye said. "And that would be me." The lawyer, who was wearing a black suit, a shoestring tie, and a flat-crown black hat, began counting the chips in front of him.

"It would appear that I have one hundred and twenty-five dollars here."

"Well, I won't need that much," Falcon said. He bought seventy-five dollars worth of chips and stacked them up in front of him.

"Are you here for the auction?" the lawyer asked as he dealt the cards. It was easy to see why Nye was ahead. He handled the cards easily, gracefully, whereas the others around the table looked awkward, even picking up the pasteboards.

"That depends," Falcon said.

"On what?" Hayford asked.

"On how much I win here."

"What does that have to do with it?"

"Well, who knows?" Falcon said. "I might get enough money to buy a few head of prime stock, then get some land just outside of town. Then, I'd start looking for a good woman to have my kids. I'd join the local chamber of commerce, and run for mayor. If that works out, I might take a seat in Congress, then, after a few terms, I'll run for President of the United States. They'll build statues of me in Washington, and put my picture on money. I can see great things from this one little card game. So you see, gentlemen, I've got to win here tonight. Why, the future of the United States may well depend on it."

Falcon said the entire speech in complete seriousness, and at first, the others around the table looked at him in complete shock.

Then, realizing that he was putting them on, they broke into loud guffaws of laughter.

"Bill, move over," Clyde said, slapping the table. "Your position as the town humorist has just been challenged."

"Hey, Suzie," Hayford called to one of the bar girls. "Did you hear this gentleman? If he wins big, he's going to be President of the United States."

Suzie looked back at Falcon, then smiled broadly. "I just heard the part where he would be looking for a wife," she said. Then, to Falcon: "Honey, you're a good-lookin' man. Maybe I had better come over there and bring you luck. And if you do all you say you're goin' to do, I'd be happy to be your wife."

Suzie's good-natured response brought more laughter.

"Don't you be bringing any more luck to this table, Suzie, unless you bring it to me," Hayford teased.

Falcon won the first hand.

"Better watch it, Nye," Clyde said. "This fella's on his way."

As the game continued, Falcon won a little more than he was losing, but he wasn't the big winner. Neither was Nye. It was almost as if, by joining the game, Falcon had changed the rules to the point that everyone seemed to be winning a bit more. That had the effect of improving everyone's mood. And as their mood improved, they began talking about how much money the auction would generate.

"Why, before this auction is over, I'll bet there'll be more money in this little town than in all of Denver," Nye said as he picked up the cards. He groaned. "Who is the idiot that dealt this terrible hand?"

"You are," Hayford said.

"I rest my case."

"Good evening, gentlemen," a woman's voice said.

There was something familiar about the voice, and turning, Falcon saw Kathleen Coyle.

"Why, Miss Coyle," he said, starting to rise. "What are you doing here?"

Kathleen chuckled. "I thought we were old friends by now," she said. "Surely you can call me Kathleen. And everyone has to be somewhere. Are you displeased to see me?"

"No, of course not," Falcon said. "It's just that I didn't expect it, that's all."

"Well, as to what I am doing here, I'm singing." She smiled broadly. "I'm finally getting to perform. Isn't that wonderful?"

"Yes, it is. I'm very pleased for you. Where

are you performing?"

"Why, right here in the Gold Strike," Kathleen said. She pointed to the piano player, who in all the time Falcon had been in the saloon had played not a note. "Jimmy is my accompanist. Jimmy, this is my friend, Falcon MacCallister."

Hayford had just taken a swallow of his beer, but upon hearing MacCallister's name, he spewed it back out over the table.

"Hayford, what the hell's got into you?" one of the other players complained, wiping the beer from the table.

"MacCallister?" Hayford said. "Did she say your name was Falcon MacCallister?"

"Yes."

"Well, I'll be," he said. "Boys, I don't know if you know it or not, but Mr. Mac-Callister here is a man of some renown. For example, along with Mickey Free, he cleaned out Naiche and his bunch a few years back. Then, if that wasn't enough, he went back down there and took care of Keytano. Yes, sir, Arizona is safe because of this man. Mr. MacCallister, I wonder if I could shake your hand."

Falcon was uncomfortable with all the accolades, but he smiled and shook Hayford's hand, then the hand of everyone he had been playing cards with, as well as the hands

138

of several others who came over to meet him.

"Say," Nye said. "You may have just been teasing about running for Congress before, but I believe I could get you elected."

"I doubt that," Falcon said. "And I was teasing."

"Don't be too sure I couldn't do it. Look what happened to Davy Crockett. He was a hero who wound up in Congress."

"Yeah," Falcon said. "He also wound up dead."

"A minor obstacle," Nye said with a dismissive wave of his hand.

The others laughed.

Falcon looked back toward Kathleen. "When do you sing again?"

"I'll sing right now if you'd like."

"Please do," Falcon invited.

"The song is called, 'A Cowboy's Wife I'll Be,' and it was written by Mr. George Henry Russel."

Kathleen nodded at the pianist, who, putting his whiskey glass on top of the piano, began to play. After the introduction, Kathleen, smiling sweetly, began to sing.

I'm a wild and laughing girl,
Just turned sweet sixteen,
As full of mischief and fun

As ever you have seen;
And when I am a woman grown,
No city beau for me.
If ever I marry in this life,
A cowboy's wife I'll be.

The song had a bouncy melody, and
Kathleen was pretty and perky and all
conversation halted as she sang. Kathleen
danced around the room, stopping first at
one table, then another. Sometimes she
would put her finger under her chin and
curtsy; other times she would throw her hip
out and pout. But at every table she had a
way of looking into the eyes of her listeners,
making it appear as if she were singing to
them, and them alone. She purposely did
not come to Falcon's table until she reached
the last verse.

Let those who like it best
Enjoy the smoky town,
Midst dusty walls and dusky walks
To ramble up and down;
But sunny fields and shady groves
Have charms enough for me.
So if ever I marry in this life
A cowboy's wife I'll be!

About eighty percent of the customers in
the saloon were cowboys, and they burst

into applause as she finished.

"Darlin', I'm the cowboy you should marry!" one of them called.

"To hell with that! I'm the one!" another shouted, and soon several were shouting out their proposals.

Kathleen laughed them off; then she walked over to the bar and held up a glass.

"Boys," she called, "will you all buy a fresh drink and have it with me?"

"I'll drink with you," one of the cowboys said.

"Me too!" another shouted, and nearly everyone in the saloon rushed to the bar for a drink or a refill.

Nye chuckled. "She does that after every song," he said. "She's been the best thing for Sylvester's business since he opened the Gold Strike."

"Do you know her from somewhere?" Hayford asked.

"I met her up in Miles City, Montana, a few weeks ago."

"And here she is in Laramie, Wyoming," Nye said. "Small world."

"Yes," Falcon agreed.

After a few more hands, Nye stood up. "Well, gentlemen, since my luck has turned, I think I'll leave the game before I lose it all back."

"I have to go as well," Hayford said. "I've got some more work to do on tomorrow's paper."

The departure of both Nye and Hayford effectively ended the game, so Falcon took his chips over to the bar and cashed them in. He had won ten dollars on the night, which ironically was the amount of money he had paid for his room and board.

Kathleen came over to stand beside him.

"What did you think of the song?" she asked.

"I thought you did very well."

Kathleen smiled, obviously pleased by his response. "I hoped you would like it," she said.

"I must say, it was a surprise, seeing you here," Falcon said.

"I'm not here by chance," she said candidly. "I heard you and Mr. Kohrs talking about what was going to happen here, and I thought it might be interesting to come down and watch. Besides, it gave me another chance to see you. Do you have a place to stay tonight?"

"Yes, I've taken a room," Falcon said.

"I've got a room here in the saloon. It comes with the job. You could always give your room up and come stay with me," she invited.

It was a tempting invitation, but Falcon didn't like to get too involved with any one woman. Since losing Marie, he was not ready to give too much of himself to any woman now.

"I thank you for the invitation," he said. He softened his rejection with a smile. "But if I'm going to be bidding on cattle, I need to keep my head clear. I'm afraid you would be too much of a distraction."

Kathleen chuckled. "I'll accept that as a compliment," she said.

"Good, because that's what I intended it to be." Tossing the rest of his drink down, Falcon told Kathleen good-bye, then left the saloon.

TEN

It was eleven P.M. when Falcon let himself into his room. He noticed that the covers were turned down for him, and a lantern burned dimly by his bedside. There was a note on the table under the lantern.

Mr. MacCallister,
I hope you enjoy your stay with us. I will be serving breakfast at seven of the morning. I will knock once lightly on your door.
Sincerely,
Frances Martin

The knock on his door the next morning wasn't gentle, but neither was it made by Mrs. Martin.

"Mr. MacCallister! Mr. MacCallister," Gordon's young voice called. "It's time for breakfast!"

Falcon opened his eyes and looked around the room. For just a moment, he was disoriented. The room was unlike any hotel room he had ever been in. Instead of a bare table and a spartan closet, this room had an ornate dresser and chest of drawers, a claw-foot table, curtains on the windows, pictures on the wall, and a carpet on the floor.

"Mr. MacCallister!" Gordon called again. "Are you awake in there?"

"Yes," Falcon said. "I'll be out in a few minutes."

"Don't be long. Mom gets sore when folks are late for breakfast."

Falcon smiled. "I'll hurry," he said.

For a moment, as Falcon was dressing, he thought back to the days when he was part of a family, getting dressed in the morning, eating around the breakfast table with his parents and siblings. Part of that feeling tugged at his heartstrings now, and made him feel pain.

But in a strange way, he also took a great deal of comfort from it, and was looking forward to having breakfast with Gordon and his mother.

The pleasant feeling continued when he passed through the kitchen into the dining room. He could smell fresh coffee, bacon, and biscuits. And when he sat down, he saw that she had made gravy.

"Oh," he said, almost in a sigh of delight.

"I can't remember the last time I had a home-cooked breakfast like this. Mrs. Martin, you are a wonder."

Frances smiled in embarrassment. "My goodness," she said. "It is just a breakfast."

"Just a breakfast? And I suppose you think the Rocky Mountains are just a few hills."

Frances laughed, the sound reminding Falcon of wind chimes.

"Gordon, would you please pass Mr. MacCallister the biscuits?" Frances said.

"Yes, ma'am," Gordon answered, passing the plate to Falcon.

As Falcon picked up a biscuit, he let his hand fly up. "Goodness," he said. "This biscuit is so light it's about to fly away."

Frances laughed again.

"Gratuitous compliments aren't necessary, Mr. MacCallister," she said. "You may have as many biscuits as you wish."

"In that case, I'll just take another while the platter is here," Falcon said, taking a second biscuit.

"Mr. MacCallister, are you going to take part in the rodeo today?" Gordon asked.

"Rodeo? What rodeo?"

"Some of the local businessmen arranged it. It's to celebrate the big cattle auction. There's going to be riding contests, roping contests, shooting contests, all sorts of things. There's going to be a footrace too, and I aim to enter that."

"Are you a good runner?"

"I'm the fastest runner in Albany County."

"Gordon, don't brag so," Frances scolded.

"It ain't braggin' if it's true," Gordon said.

"It *isn't* bragging if it's true," Frances corrected.

"See, even you think that."

"I was correcting your grammar," Frances said.

"All right, but I am the fastest runner in Albany County," Gordon said.

"I wish you luck in the race," Falcon said.

"Thanks, but I don't need it. I'm going to win," Gordon said resolutely.

"Gordon, bragging is not an admirable trait," Frances said.

"But confidence is," Falcon said. "And I admire the young man's confidence."

Back in Denver, Gilly Cardis had just about given up trying to find Falcon MacCallister. It was early morning of his third day in Denver, and he had spent the previous two days wandering around town, picking people at random to ask where MacCallister lived. An amazing number of people knew about MacCallister, but no one knew him, and not one person could tell Cardis

147

where Falcon lived.

Having just finished breakfast, he was about to start on another day of looking for MacCallister when he happened across a young newspaper boy.

"Paper! Get your morning paper!" the boy was shouting, holding up the paper so people could see the headlines.

As Cardis walked by, one of the stories caught his eye.

CATTLE AUCTION IN LARAMIE.
Falcon MacCallister Among Those In Attendance.

Cardis grabbed the paper to look at it.

"Hey, mister, that'll be five cents!" the newspaper boy said indignantly.

"I just want to see this one story," Cardis said.

"It will cost you five cents," the boy said again. "Unless you want me to call that policeman over."

Looking up, Cardis noticed that a policeman was standing on the corner and, having overheard the paperboy, was now looking back toward him.

"All right, here's your nickel," Cardis said irritably.

The boy handed the paper to Cardis, and

Cardis looked more closely at the story that had caught his attention.

CATTLE AUCTION IN LARAMIE.
Falcon MacCallister Among Those In Attendance.
NEW BREED OF CATTLE TO BE AUCTIONED.
To be attended by America's Wealthiest Cattle Barons,
Colorado to be Represented by MacCallister.
Upwards of 100,000 Dollars to be Spent!
Said to be end of the Longhorn.

Cardis read no further than the headline and sub-headlines. He didn't need to. If Falcon MacCallister was in Laramie, then that was where he was going as well.

He handed the paper back to the boy.

"All right," he said. "I've read it. Give me my nickel back."

"I'm sorry, mister, you bought it," the paperboy said. "It's your paper now."

"Give me my nickel back, you little shit, or I'll pound your head in," Cardis said angrily.

The paperboy took out a coin, then dropped it. As Cardis bent over to pick it

149

up, the paperboy ran. That was when Cardis saw that the boy had returned a penny, not a nickel.

The boy was too fast and had too much of a head start for Cardis to be able to do anything. Angrily, he threw the paper down on the street, then walked quickly to the depot.

It was still early morning, but the depot was as crowded now as it had been when he arrived. He had no idea how many people were milling around, but he believed that this depot alone had as many people as most of the towns he was familiar with.

He could feel, almost as much as hear, the heavy trains moving around out in the train shed. Someone was standing by the door that led TO TRAINS, shouting through a megaphone.

"Train for Kansas City and points east, now loading on Track Five!"

Cardis walked over to the long counter with the frosted glass. He stepped up to one of the windows.

"Yes, sir, how may I help you?"

"How much is a ticket to Laramie?" he asked.

"Four dollars."

"When is the next train?"

"The next train to Laramie is sitting on

Track Three at this very moment," the ticket agent said. "If you hurry, you can catch it. It will put you in Laramie by eight o'clock this evening."

"Give me a ticket," Cardis said, presenting his money to the agent.

At the very moment Gilly Cardis was boarding the train in Denver, the entire town of Laramie, Wyoming, was turned out for the festivities. Bleachers had been erected around the corral, and the spectators cheered for their favorites as cowboys from neighboring ranches competed for best rider. The riding and roping events took up most of the morning; then people began gathering for the footrace. The runners were loosening up, kicking their legs high, running quick sprints, then coming back to the starting line. There were at least twenty entered in the race, and Gordon was clearly the youngest.

Frances was standing behind her son, massaging his neck and shoulders.

"Mr. MacCallister, are you going to enter the shooting match this afternoon?" Gordon asked.

"I don't know," Falcon said. "I haven't thought about it."

"I think you should enter."

"Gordon, Mr. MacCallister can make up his own mind whether or not he enters," Frances said.

"If I win this race, will you enter?" Gordon asked.

"You don't have to win. It's enough that you are competing," MacCallister said.

"Ha!" Gordon replied. "You are just saying that because you don't think I can win and you don't want me to feel bad."

Falcon smiled. "Something like that," he agreed.

"Well, don't worry. I'm going to win."

"How long is this race?"

"It's to the fork in the river and back."

"How far is that?"

"Three miles to the fork, so the race is six miles."

Falcon let out a whistle. "You are going to run for six miles?"

"Yep."

"Gordon?" Frances said.

Gordon smiled sheepishly. "I mean, yes, sir."

"People, people, people!" a loud voice called. "All runners for the footrace, come to the starting line now!"

"I've got to go," Gordon said.

"Good luck," Falcon called to the boy as he sprinted back to the starting line.

The official starter got all the runners lined up behind the starting line, then explained that he would start them by firing his pistol in the air.

Falcon looked at the line of runners. Gordon was clearly the youngest, and the smallest.

"Look at him," Frances said. "So young and so sure of himself." She sighed. "I do hope he does well."

The gun popped and the runners started. Although Falcon knew that the start of a distance race wasn't as explosive as the start of a sprint, he knew that it was just as important, for there was an immediate jockeying for position as the field began setting up. Before they passed the church at the edge of town, there were already frequent changes of leadership among the top six runners.

As the runners grew smaller in the distance, the field was fairly well strung out. But because Gordon was clearly the shortest of all the runners, he could be identified, even at this distance. He was running in the front one third of the pack.

Then they were too far to make out at all.

"Oh," Frances said nervously. "I wish we could see them."

"We'll just have to wait until . . ." Falcon

began; then glancing across the street, he saw something in the window of the hardware store that made him smile. "Wait a minute," he said. "I'll be right back."

A bell hanging from the door announced Falcon's entrance into the hardware store. A clerk came to greet him.

"Yes, sir?"

"I want to buy that," Falcon said, pointing to the object in the window.

"Yes, sir," the clerk said, tending to the transaction.

A moment later Falcon went back outside and, taking Frances by the arm, said, "Come with me."

"Come with you where?"

"Up here, where we can see Gordon," Falcon said. He led her up a set of stairs that climbed the side of the apothecary. At the top of the stairs was a small porch that was the entrance to the doctor's office. There, Falcon removed his purchase from the sack. It was a pair of binoculars. He looked through them, then handed them to Frances.

"Can you see him?" he asked.

"Yes!" Frances said, smiling broadly. "Thank you!"

She looked through them for a minute, then said, "Oh, look! Gordon is running very well!"

She handed them to Falcon, who raised them to his eyes to check out the field.

By now, the first three runners had opened up a significant lead on the rest of the pack. In fact, some of the runners had already stopped running and were walking. As the first three reached the fork in the river, they made their turn and started back. Gordon was running number three, but was hanging very close to the first two runners.

The three leaders were coming back now, passing many of the runners who had not yet made it to the fork in the river. As they came closer, they came back into view and the town could see them. Many began cheering for their favorite.

"Oh, Gordon, run, sweetheart, run!" Frances said. Her urging was passionate and genuine, even though she said it so quietly that only Falcon could hear her.

The three reached the edge of town, and were less than two hundred yards from the finish. Then Gordon put on a burst of speed, surprising the two runners in front of him. He took the lead just as they passed the church, then began opening up the lead until he crossed the finish line at least ten yards ahead of the second-place runner.

By now the crowd was cheering loudly for

Gordon, impressed not only by his youth, but by his athleticism. Several of the men rushed to him and lifted him onto their shoulders. The laurel wreath of victory was passed up to him and he put it on his head, then waved to the crowd. Finding Falcon and his mother in the crowd, he shouted.

"I won the race, Mr. MacCallister! That means you have to enter the shooting match!"

Falcon laughed. "I didn't take you up on your bet, Gordon," he said. "But I'll enter."

Eleven

Three wagons, loaded with bales of hay, were maneuvered into position, the drivers of the wagons expertly handling the two-mule teams that were pulling them. The wagons completely blocked off the main road coming into town, and riders were sent at least a mile down the road to prevent anyone from wandering into the line of fire.

Each wagon had four targets attached to the hay bales, so that a total of twelve targets were ready for the shooters in the competition.

Twenty-four shooters were entered, which meant there would be two heats, the top six of each heat selected to move on to the next round.

Deputy Sheriff Seth Joyner was in charge of the shooting match, and when all was ready, he gave the call. "Shooters, into your stalls!"

Falcon was in the first heat, so he picked

up his Winchester.

"Good luck," Frances said.

"Thanks."

The shooting positions were stalls, exactly as the judge had called them. Each stall was separated from the other by a wall of canvas.

"Present your weapons for inspection now. Remember, they must be empty," Joyner said.

One of the judges came up to Falcon and held out his hand, asking for the rifle. Falcon put the lever down to open the breach, then presented the weapon to the judge. The judge cycled through a few times, then handed the rifle back to Falcon. He also gave him three .30-caliber bullets.

"Do not load until Deputy Joyner gives the orders to do so," the judge explained.

Falcon nodded, and held the three bullets in his hand.

"Shooters," Deputy Joyner called. "Load your weapons!"

Falcon loaded the three bullets.

"After you receive the order to fire, you will have one minute to shoot all three bullets," Joyner said.

Falcon waited.

"Commence firing at your discretion," Joyner called.

Falcon raised the rifle to his shoulder and

sighted down the barrel. The targets were only seventy-five yards away, an incredibly easy shot for Falcon. He fired all three shots as quickly as he could operate the lever.

Falcon was one of the six selected to go on to the next round, and he left the stall, carrying his weapon with him. He saw Gordon, but he didn't see Frances.

"Where's your mom?" Falcon asked.

"She's around here somewhere," Gordon said.

Six shooters were chosen from the second round as well so that, once again, twelve shooters moved up to the firing line.

The twelve were cut to six for the third round. All six in the third round tied, so the judges moved the wagons back again. This time only four survived. After another round, only Falcon and one other shooter remained. The other shooter was at the far end of the shooting line, shielded from Falcon's view by the canvas walls.

With only two shooters left, Joyner changed the rules slightly. Now, instead of shooting only three rounds, they were given seven rounds to shoot.

"Target number one: seven bulls. Target number twelve: seven bulls," the down-range judge called back up to the shooting line.

The targets were moved, then moved again. They were now three hundred yards away.

"Commence firing!" Deputy Joyner said.

Falcon raised his rifle to his shoulder, fired, jacked a round into the chamber, fired again, then repeated the process until he had fired seven times.

After both shooters were finished, someone went out to check the targets. Again, each shooter had scored seven bull's-eyes.

"It looks like we might be here all night," Joyner said. The spectators, and now there were several, laughed.

"Deputy, I have an idea, if the other shooter is agreeable," Falcon said.

"Let's hear it," Joyner replied.

"How about having us fire one at a time?" Falcon suggested. "Time how long it takes us to fire seven shots. Whoever gets the highest score in the least time wins."

Harper went down to check with the other shooter, then came back to Falcon. "It's acceptable," he said.

Falcon nodded, picked up his rifle, then waited for Joyner to shout, "Now."

Falcon began firing, jacking each additional round in so quickly that he sometimes had two ejected cartridges in the air at the same time. After seven shots he lowered his rifle.

"Five-and-one-half seconds," the timer said.

A judge down-range checked his hits. Then a rider galloped back with the report.

"Seven bull's-eyes."

"Seven bulls in five-and-one-half seconds," Deputy Joyner said. He shook his head. "Mister, that is some shooting."

Falcon waited for the other shooter. He tried to keep count of the seconds, and estimated that every round had been fired in about six seconds.

"Six-and-one-half seconds," the timer said, confirming Falcon's estimate.

Falcon and the crowd waited for the rider to return from down range with the target report. Joyner looked at it, nodded, then shouted.

"Seven bull's-eyes! Ladies and gentlemen, based on time, we have a winner!" He pointed to Falcon, and the crowd applauded.

"I would like to congratulate the man I was shooting against," Falcon said. "That was some very good shooting."

Frances Martin stepped out from behind the canvas wall, carrying a Winchester.

"What makes you think you were shooting against a man?" she asked, smiling sweetly.

"You?" Falcon asked. "I was shooting against you?"

Gordon laughed. "I should have told you about her, but I wanted to see if you were a better shot than my mom."

"I'm not a better shot than she is," Falcon said. "I just got lucky."

"No," Frances said. "You beat me by a full second. That isn't luck, that is skill."

"Where did you learn to shoot like that?" Falcon asked.

"From my father," Frances said. "He was a wonderful shot. He wanted to prove that he could train a woman to shoot as well as a man."

"I would say that he proved his point," Falcon said.

"Congratulations, Falcon," another woman's voice said, and turning, Falcon saw Kathleen approaching, smiling prettily at him.

"Oh," Falcon said. "Thank you."

"Aren't you going to introduce me to your friend?" Kathleen asked. "Don't worry, I'm not jealous."

"Jealous?" Frances asked, raising her eyebrows. "I assure you, miss, you have no reason to be jealous."

"Oh, don't get me wrong," Kathleen said. "It's just that Falcon and I are old friends. We knew each other back in Miles City."

"I see," Frances said. "Well, we had better be getting home. Come along, Gordon."

"Oh, Mom, can't I . . . ?"

"Come along," Frances said again.

"Yes, ma'am."

"Oh, dear," Kathleen said as Frances and Gordon walked away. "I do hope I didn't cause any trouble."

"No trouble," Falcon said. "She owns the boardinghouse where I am staying."

"Oh, I see. Well, like I said, I do hope I didn't cause any trouble." She smiled brightly. "But I wanted to tell you the good news."

"What good news?"

"I'm doing a show tonight."

"Then I shall present myself at the Gold Strike to watch your performance."

Kathleen shook her head. "No, that's what's good about the news. It isn't at the Gold Strike," she said. "It's at the Royale Theater. I'm doing a special show for all the cattle buyers who are in town. Then, afterward, there will be a party at the Gold Strike. You will come, won't you?"

"Yes, of course I'll come," Falcon said.

"You won't disappoint me now? Because

while I'm on stage, I'll be looking for you. And if I don't see you, why, I don't know if I will be able to finish my performance or not."

"I'll be there," Falcon promised.

After Kathleen left, Falcon hurried after Frances, but he didn't catch up to her until he reached the house.

"Why did you hurry off?" he asked.

"I didn't want to intrude," Frances said.

"You weren't intruding at all."

"Well, perhaps not. But I don't like to get into the personal lives of any of my guests. It's not the best thing to do."

"Mrs. Martin . . . Frances," Falcon said. "You don't understand. It's not like that."

"So you didn't know her in Miles City?"

"Well, yes, I knew her in Miles City. That's where I met her."

"So your relationship there was . . . casual?"

Falcon remembered Kathleen coming into his hotel room on the night of the cattlemen's ball. As he thought of it, he flushed slightly, and Kathleen noticed.

"I'm sorry," she said quickly, holding her hand up. "I had no right to ask such a question. Please, forgive me for that."

"There is nothing to forgive," Falcon said. "Uh, look, the reason Kathleen came over to speak to me is because she is doing a show tonight at the Royale Theater. She is a very good singer. Maybe you would like to attend the show with me?"

Frances shook her head. "No," she said. "I'd better not."

"I think you would enjoy it," Falcon said.

Frances pinched the bridge of her nose. "Please, Mr. MacCallister . . . Falcon," she said, softening her tone. She took her hand away from her nose and smiled at him. "Please don't misunderstand. I'm not upset with you, nor am I reading anything into your relationship with Miss Coyle. But it has been a long and busy day for me. I think I had better stay home. Besides, I should start your supper."

"No," Falcon said. Then, when he saw her reaction to his comment, he smiled to put her at ease. "They are going to have a party at the Gold Strike after the show. There will be food there. You needn't bother tonight."

"Are you sure? You have paid for it, you know."

"I'm sure," Falcon said. "I'll see you at breakfast."

"All right," Frances said.

Frances waited until Falcon was gone; then she turned to her son and smiled at him.

165

"Well, my champion runner," she said, "what can I fix you? What would you like more than anything else?"

"Fried peach pies," Gordon said.

"For dessert? Very well, fried peach pies it will be."

Gordon shook his head. "No, not for dessert," he said. "For supper."

"Fried peach pies? That's all you want?"

"Yes, ma'am."

"Well, all right. You did win your race today, and I did promise to fix whatever you liked."

"Mom?"

"What?" Frances asked as she got down a can of peaches.

"Are you in love with Mr. MacCallister?"

"What?" Frances gasped. "Of course not! Whatever gave you such an idea?"

"It's just the way you were talkin' to him," Gordon said. "It was like you didn't care much for that pretty woman that come to talk to him. The one he is goin' to go hear sing."

"Well, I — I was just surprised that he had known her before, that's all. I mean, we're a long way from Miles City. It seemed like an unusual coincidence."

"That sure would be good, though."

"What would be good?"

"It would be good if you were in love with Mr. MacCallister and you got married. Then Falcon MacCallister would be my dad."

"No!" Frances said, looking at her son and shaking her head. "Your father was Loomis Martin. He was a very fine man, and a railroad engineer. You should be very proud of him."

"I am proud of him," Gordon said. He was silent for a moment. "But I wish he was here with us right now."

"I wish that as well," Frances said. "But just because he isn't with us in person, doesn't mean he isn't with us. I expect he is looking out for us right now."

Gordon smiled broadly. "Do you think he knows I won the race today?"

Frances chuckled, and nodded her head. "I'm sure he knows," she said.

TWELVE

"Laramie," the conductor called out. "This is Laramie."

Cardis looked through the window as the Laramie station came into view. Although not a huge metropolis as Denver had been, Laramie was considerably larger than most of the towns of his experience.

Stepping down from the train, he saw someone standing on the station platform, wearing the hat of a railroad official and looking at his watch.

"Hey," Cardis said to him. "I'm a'lookin' for a man named MacCallister. You know whereat I can find him?"

Cody Martin looked at the man who was inquiring about MacCallister. There was something about him that made Cody feel uneasy . . . too uneasy to tell him that the man he was looking for was staying in his sister-in-law's house.

Cody shook his head. "You might find him at the Gold Strike."

"The Gold Strike?"

"It's a saloon, just up the street," Cody said. "You can't miss it. It's the only one in town."

"Thanks."

Cardis followed the stationmaster's directions to the saloon. He was surprised to see that it was practically empty, and the only two people there were stringing bunting around. A big sign on one of the walls read:

CONGRATULATIONS TO KATHLEEN
COYLE,
OUR SONGBIRD

"Hold that end up, will you, Clyde?" one of the two men said to the other.

Cardis stepped up to the bar and slapped his hand down on it.

"You got yourself a customer, Sylvester," Clyde said.

"I'll be right with you," Sylvester said. He was standing on a chair, tacking up one end of a red, white, and blue bunting, while Clyde was holding his end to the wall.

"I want a beer," Cardis called back.

"Well, help yourself," Sylvester said. "Just leave a nickel on the bar."

Cardis went around behind the bar, picked up a mug, and drew about a quarter of a glass of beer. Then, seeing that neither of the men were looking at him, he swallowed his beer quickly and refilled his mug.

"Where is ever'body?" he asked, coming back around to the front of the bar, carrying his beer. "I ain't never seen a saloon this empty at this time of night."

"Why, they are all at the show," Clyde said. "Sylvester, you'd better put another tack in it; that don't look like it's goin' to hold."

"This'll hold it," Sylvester said.

"Well, you're the boss, but if it was me, I'd put another tack in it," Clyde said.

"What show?" Cardis capped his question with a swallow of his beer.

Sylvester pointed to the sign. "The show Miss Coyle is giving," he said. "This is where she works, but tonight she's down at the Royale, giving a special show for all the cattle buyers."

"The cattle buyers? What cattle buyers?"

"Where've you been, mister?" Clyde asked. "You don't know about the big cattle auction we're about to have?"

"Oh, yeah," Cardis said. "I think I did hear somethin' about that." He recalled the headlines he had read that brought him to

170

Laramie. He didn't read the story, but the headlines had mentioned something about cattle. "That's what Falcon MacCallister come here for, ain't it? To buy cattle?"

"MacCallister? Yes, I believe it is," Clyde said.

"So he's here then? MacCallister?"

"Well, no, he ain't here," Sylvester said. "Use your eyes. Me'n Clyde's the only ones here."

"I mean is he here in town?"

"Oh, yes, he's in town all right," Sylvester said. "In fact, he won a shooting match today. I swear, I never saw anyone who could shoot like that. I mean, he beat Frances Martin. I didn't think anyone could do that."

"He killed this Martin fella, did he?"

Sylvester chuckled. "Frances Martin ain't a fella, she's a woman. And no, he didn't kill her. It wasn't anything like that. This was a shooting match, shooting at targets."

"You think MacCallister will be in here later tonight?"

"Oh, yes, I'm sure of it," Sylvester said.

It was the last song of the show, and Kathleen stepped to the front of the stage to speak to the audience.

"You have all been so wonderful tonight,

and I have enjoyed singing the songs you have requested. But I am going to sing this last song for me. It was written by a man named Thomas P. Westendorf, and when you hear it, you will know why it has such meaning for me."

Kathleen looked over at the orchestra leader and nodded. He raised his baton, and the music began to play. As Kathleen sang her song, she looked directly at Falcon.

I'll take you home again, Kathleen,
Across the ocean wild and wide,
To where your heart has ever been,
Since first you were my bonny bride.
The roses all have left your cheek,
I've watched them fade away and die;
Your voice is sad whene'er you speak,
And tears bedim your loving eyes.
Oh! I will take you back, Kathleen,
To where your heart will feel no pain,
And when the fields are fresh and green,
I'll take you to your home again.

When the song ended, Kathleen acknowledged the applause; then, as the curtains began to close, she held up her hand to stop them, and stepped out to the front of the stage again.

"We are having a celebration over at the

Gold Strike, and I invite all of you to come join us."

With a final curtsy, she retreated back behind the closing curtains as the audience stood and began to file out of the theater.

One of the stagehands came out into the audience and found Falcon as he was talking to Kohrs and some of the other cattlemen.

"Mr. MacCallister?" the stagehand said.

"Yes."

"Miss Coyle's compliments, sir, and she asks if you would wait long enough to escort her over to the Gold Strike."

"I think quite an impression on the lady you have made," Kohrs said, laughing.

"So it would seem," Falcon said. He wasn't particularly pleased that she had asked him to wait for her, but he decided it would be rude to turn her down.

"What shall I tell her?" the stagehand asked.

Sighing, Falcon sat back down. "Tell her I will wait right here for her," he said.

"Very good, sir."

Back at the Gold Strike, Gilly Cardis was on his third beer by the time the crowd started arriving from the theater. They were laughing and talking, and while several of them hurried to the bar, the others found tables and, within a few minutes, the saloon changed from being empty and quiet to crowded and noisy.

"I'm tellin' you, she's a pure nightingale, that girl is," one of the arriving customers was saying. "I ain't never heard no one who could sing as pretty as that."

"Why, she sings in here most ever' night," one of the others said. "So I could'a told you before this here concert ever come about how pretty a singer she is."

"She ain't just a pretty singer; she's a pretty girl too, and that's a fact."

"Yeah, but it won't do no good for any of us to get any ideas. She has a fancy for Mac-Callister," the first man said.

Hearing MacCallister's name mentioned, Cardis moved closer to them so he could overhear their conversation.

"How do you know she has a fancy for him?"

" 'Cause, I was sittin' right behind Mac-Callister and Mr. Kohrs for the whole show. I figured something was up, the way she kept lookin' over toward him while she was singin'. Then, soon's the show was over, a stagehand come out and ask MacCallister to wait for her. He's over there now."

"Are you sure? The theater's empty now,

ain't it?"

"Not entirely empty. MacCallister's over there now, sittin' out in the dark, just waitin' for her."

The other man laughed. "Can you imagine someone like Falcon MacCallister sittin' in the dark like that just because some woman asked him to?"

"Yeah, well, there's no tellin' what all a man will do for a pretty woman. Even a man like Falcon MacCallister."

The gas lamps in the theater had been extinguished except for the one closest to Falcon. The theater staff left it burning because they knew that he was waiting for Kathleen. Falcon pulled his watch from his pocket and checked it. He had been waiting for her for one half hour. How long did it take her to get ready anyway?

Cardis tried the front door of the theater and found that it was unlocked. He let himself in, then moved quietly through the lobby and into the orchestra seating area. As soon as he stepped into the orchestra area, he saw a single light glowing down front, near the stage. And he saw a man standing near the light.

Cardis drew his pistol, aimed carefully,

then pulled the trigger.

The sound of the gunshot sounded very loud in the closed, darkened, and quiet confines of the theater. Through the billowing cloud of gun smoke, Cardis saw the man he had shot at clutch his chest, then fall.

"MacCallister! My name is Gilly Cardis and I got you, you son of a bitch!" he shouted. "That's for killing my brother!"

Suddenly someone stood up from one of the seats.

"I'm MacCallister!" he shouted. "You shot an innocent man, Cardis!"

"No!" Cardis shouted as he turned to run from the theater.

With his gun drawn, Falcon ran out of the theater after him.

A couple of people were standing in front of the theater. They had heard a shot, and they saw someone run from the theater; now they saw Falcon coming out holding a pistol.

"What's going on?" one of them asked.

Falcon recognized Hayford, the publisher of the town newspaper.

"Hayford, get the doc quick," Falcon said. "That man just shot one of the stagehands."

"He ran to the other side of the track!" one of the others said. This was Nye, the lawyer.

A gunshot sounded from the other side of the track, and Falcon heard someone shout. Falcon started toward the track on the run; then he saw someone coming out of the darkness toward him. It was Deputy Joyner.

"Joyner, did you see him? Which way did he go?" Falcon asked.

Falcon saw a circle of fire on Joyner's coat.

"Damn!" Joyner said, his voice strained with pain. "Damn, this hurts."

Joyner fell facedown. Falcon ran over to him and rolled the deputy over. He patted out the ring of fire on his jacket. That was when he realized what had caused the fire in the first place. Deputy Joyner had been shot at point-blank range, and the powder blast from the revolver had set his jacket ablaze.

As he knelt over the deputy, Falcon could hear the sound of an approaching train.

"Joyner? Joyner, can you hear me?" Falcon asked the deputy.

Joyner moved his lips as if trying to speak, but was unable to. He took two more ragged gasps; then he stopped breathing. Falcon put his hand to the young deputy's neck, feeling for a pulse. There was none.

The train sounded closer.

"Deputy Joyner, he's over here!" a man's voice called from the other side of the tracks, and Falcon, with his pistol drawn, ran across the track and saw Cody Martin.

"Where's Deputy Joyner?" Cody asked when he saw Falcon.

"He's dead," Falcon replied. "Cody, did you see the man who shot him?"

"I think I did. At least, I saw a man holding a gun running that way," Cody said, pointing toward one of the railroad signs.

"Thanks," Falcon said. Looking back up the track, he saw that the train had already reached the far end of town. "Cody, you'd better get back to the depot and get those people out of the way."

"Yeah, good idea," Cody said.

Falcon started in the direction Cody had pointed, but it was too dark to see anything. As he got closer, though, he could hear heavy breathing. He listened for any sound of movement, but there was none. Whoever he was after was remaining very still.

Now the train was so close that its headlight beam began to light up the area, and in the darkness alongside the track, it picked up the gleam of a spur rowel.

"I see you!" Falcon shouted. "Come toward me with your hands up, or I'll shoot!"

"Not as good as I can see you!" the man

called, and Falcon realized then that he was being backlit by the headlamp of the train.

The man fired at Falcon, and he heard the bullet fly past his ear. Using the gunman's muzzle flash as a target, he returned fire.

At the precise moment Falcon fired, the train was coming around a small bend, which brought its light to bear on Falcon's adversary. Falcon saw the gunman suddenly throw up his gun, then fall backward, sliding headfirst down the railroad embankment. Now he was lying in the light of the train, which was pulling into the station no more than fifty yards behind them. Falcon could hear the squeal of brakes and the sound of steam being vented through relief valves. The bell was clanging loudly.

Falcon ran to his would-be assassin, and as he stood over him, he saw bubbles of blood coming from the man's mouth. The wounded man was trying hard to breathe, and Falcon heard a sucking sound in his chest. He knew then that his bullet had penetrated the man's lungs.

"Gilly Cardis?"

"Yeah."

"I thought you were in prison."

"I didn't like it all that much, so I left," Cardis said. Despite the seriousness of his wound, he couldn't help but chuckle at his own dry humor. He paid for the laughter, though, by an episode of sporadic coughing, which he found very painful.

"You would have been better off if you had stayed."

"Yeah, it looks like it, doesn't it?" Cardis said. "Who was it I shot back there?"

"You shot the deputy."

"No, I mean in the theater. Who was it I shot in the theater?"

"You shot a stagehand."

"Damn. I thought I was shootin' you." He took a few more rasping breaths. "Ain't that a hell of a note?"

Falcon didn't answer.

"I'm dyin', ain't I?"

"Yes," Falcon replied flatly.

There had been several people on the depot platform awaiting the arrival of the train, and though Cody had managed to get them out of the way temporarily, they'd seen Falcon's adversary go down in the light of the train. Now they surged down the track to be firsthand witnesses to the drama that was playing out before them.

"Where is he?" one of them shouted.

"He's up there, lying alongside the track," another said. "MacCallister shot him."

"Get a rope. Let's string the son of a bitch up!"

"No need for anything like that," Falcon said.

"What do you mean there's no need? The son of a bitch killed two men. Are you saying he don't deserve to hang?"

"No, I'm saying no need for a rope. He'll be dead before you can even find one."

"MacCallister's right," another said as he looked down at Cardis. "In fact, he's already dead."

People continued to come up the track from the depot, some of them gathering around the body of Cardis, while others gathered around Deputy Joyner. Falcon was surprised to see that not only were many of the train passengers among the morbidly curious, but so was the train crew, as he saw the engineer, fireman, and conductor standing in the crowd.

"Make way! Make way here!" an authoritative voice called, and Falcon looked around to see Sheriff Rodney Gibson coming, parting the crowd before him like Moses parted the sea.

"What happened here, what's all the . . . ?" He paused when he saw his young deputy lying on the ground. He knelt beside him. "Oh, damn," he said quietly.

"He's dead, Sheriff," Falcon said.

"Who shot him?"

"That fella up there shot him," Cody Martin said, pointing to another body just up the track.

"Is that fella dead?" Sheriff Gibson asked.

"Yes," Falcon said.

"You shot him?"

Falcon nodded.

"Do you know who he is?"

"Yeah, I know. His name is Gilly Cardis."

"Gilly Cardis," Sheriff Gibson said. He shook his head. "I've never heard of him."

"He escaped from Yuma Territorial Prison," Falcon said.

"Yuma? In Arizona? What's he doing way up here in Laramie?"

"He came here to kill me," Falcon said.

"I see," he said. "He came to Laramie to kill you; instead he kills two of our people."

"I'm sorry," Falcon said.

Sheriff Gibson shook his head. "Don't be," he said. "It wasn't your fault. And at least you killed the son of a bitch. Cody?"

"Yes, sir?"

"Get these people and this train out of here. I'll get Nunlee to come over to pick up the bodies."

"Yes, sir," Cody said. "Come on, people, you heard the sheriff. Cephus," he said to the conductor. "Get your train loaded and get it out of here."

"Board!" the conductor shouted, starting back up the track toward the standing train.

"C.G.," the engineer said to his fireman, "did you let the steam die?"

"Yeah, but don't worry, Austin, I can get it back up in no time," C.G. said.

The crowd moved back up to the depot, leaving only Sheriff Gibson and Falcon behind. Both men were standing over Joyner's body.

"I'm going to have to tell his folks," Gibson said. He sighed. "That ain't somethin' I'm lookin' forward to."

Thirteen

If someone had wagered that the triple killing that evening would put a damper on the party at the Gold Strike, they would have lost the wager. If anything, the excitement of the shooting added to the excitement of the party.

Sylvester called for, and got, a moment of silence to remember Paul Mobley, the young stagehand, and Seth Joyner, the deputy.

"And three cheers for the man who brought the killer down!" Sylvester called.

"Hip, hip!"

"Hooray!"

"Hip, hip!"

"Hooray!"

"Hip, hip!"

"Hooray!"

Again, toasts were drunk, and several people came over to offer to buy Falcon a drink. He wasn't all that enthused about having people celebrating the fact that he had shot and killed someone, but he took the accolades as gracefully as he could.

Suddenly there was a loud popping noise, followed by a woman's shout of fear and pain. Looking toward the sound, they saw that a big man had just slapped Suzie.

"You bitch! You have been watering my drink, haven't you?" the big man yelled angrily.

"I don't water the drinks," Suzie said. "I don't even pour them. All I do is drink with the customers."

The man slapped her again. "Don't lie to me, bitch!"

"She's tellin' the truth, Carney," Kathleen said.

The big man pointed to Kathleen. "You stay out of this, unless you want some of the same."

"Here!" Falcon shouted, starting toward the commotion. "You leave the women alone!"

The belligerent customer was a big man, with broad shoulders and powerful arms. He turned to look toward Falcon.

"I've heard of you," he said. "You're the one they call Falcon MacCallister, ain't you?"

"I am MacCallister."

"Well, Mr. MacCallister, what are you buttin' into this for? Is this here whore your girlfriend or something?"

By now, Kathleen had taken Suzie away from the big man. She put her arms around the girl to comfort her.

Faloon saw that Suzie was safe now, and he turned to the bartender.

"Sylvester, I don't mean to be throwing out your customers, but I intend to throw this man out. I think it would be best for everyone if he left."

"You'll get no argument from me," Sylvester said.

"Oh, so you are going to throw me out, are you? And how are you going to do that? Are you going to shoot me, like you did that fella tonight? Is that how you fight? By shooting people you don't agree with?"

"Hold on there, mister," Sylvester said. "Where do you get off sayin' somethin' like that? Practically the whole town seen what happened. MacCallister didn't have any choice. Besides, the man he killed had already killed two of our own."

"I'm just sayin' that Falcon MacCallister is a big man as long as he's got a gun in his hand. I wonder how big a man he would be without it."

"My pa told me a long time ago that I

was as big as I needed to be," Falcon said.

The big man smiled, showing uneven, tobacco-stained teeth. "So," he said. "You think you're big enough to fight me?"

"If that's what it takes," Falcon said. "But I'd rather us handle this peacefully by you just walking out of here."

The big man turned as if he were leaving. Then, suddenly, he whirled back around and threw a surprise roundhouse right at Falcon.

Sensing it coming, Falcon ducked, then countered with a left jab to the big man's nose. He was well set and he hit the big man squarely. The nose went flat, and almost immediately began to swell. The big man let out a bellow of pain, and a trickle of blood started down across his lips.

"You want to stop this now?" Falcon asked.

"I'm going to knock your block off!" the big man yelled in anger.

"It doesn't look like I'm going to get on your good side, does it," Falcon said.

The big man swung another roundhouse right, missing with it as well, and this time Falcon caught him with a right hook to the chin. The hook rocked the big man back, but didn't knock him down.

Thinking the big man was on his last legs,

Falcon moved in to finish him, but was surprised that the big man had some fight left in him. Carney threw a right jab that caught Falcon squarely in the eye. Falcon's knees buckled, and he staggered back a few steps, but he didn't go down.

With a triumphant yell, the big man moved in for the kill, but that was where he made his big mistake. A roundhouse right that he intended to finish Falcon with missed, and that left the big man wide open. Falcon stepped in and threw a hard left jab to the big man's stomach. The big man let out a loud "ooof," then doubled over with his hands clasped over his belly.

That set him up, and Falcon dropped him with a hard right cross.

The crowd in the saloon cheered loudly as the big man fell, then laughed as Sylvester poured a glass of beer on him. The man coughed and sputtered, then awkwardly climbed to his feet. Unsteadily, he lifted his hands again.

Falcon made fists of his hands and got set to throw another punch, but the big man lowered his hands and just stared at Falcon.

"Is it over?" Falcon asked.

Breathing hard, the man nodded, and held up his hand palm out. "Yeah," he said. "It's over." He bent over and put his hands on his knees, then stood there for a long time, breathing hard.

"You know what I think?" Sylvester said, looking at the big man. "I think you should leave now."

Nodding, the big man started toward the door.

"Wait," Falcon said.

The big man stopped.

"Don't bother to come back," Falcon told him.

"Humph," the big man snorted. "With watered whiskey and ugly women, who would want to come back to this place anyway?" Then, pulling together what dignity he had remaining, he pushed his way out through the batwing doors.

Another round of cheers followed the big man's exit; then Kathleen stepped up to Falcon.

"How is Suzie?" Falcon asked.

"She's fine," Kathleen said. She put her finger on Falcon's eye, which was already swelling from the one good blow the big man had landed. "In fact, she probably won't have as much of a bruise as you're going to have. I was so frightened for you," she said.

"Nothing to be frightened about," Falcon said. "The worst that could have happened would have been a beating. And I've had a few of those in my life."

"Not very many, I bet," Kathleen said. "I mean, if you could handle Carney the way you did, it seems to me like you could handle just about anyone. He is a very big man."

"Carney? Is that his name? You know him?"

Kathleen shook her head. "Not really," she said. "But he's been in here a couple of times, and I've heard his name."

"Really? He's been in here?" Sylvester asked.

"Yes, a few times," Kathleen answered.

"Hmm. I don't remember ever seeing him. But if tonight is any indication, he's not the kind of man I'd care to remember anyway."

"As far as I know, he's never gotten rough with any of the girls before," Kathleen said.

"I wonder what got him so riled up tonight," Falcon asked.

"Oh, people like Carney don't need an excuse to be riled up," Kathleen said. "He's just a big bully. I was glad to see him get his comeuppance."

Falcon touched his eye, then jerked his hand back at the tenderness of the wound.

"I don't mind saying that I could have

done without the exercise," Falcon said.

Again, Kathleen put her hand on Falcon's eye. "Ohh," she said. "That looks like it hurts."

"It does hurt."

Putting her mouth close to Falcon's ear, and speaking so softly that only he could hear, Kathleen said, "Falcon, I have a room upstairs with a double bed. Why don't you come up for a while? I could —" She paused, then said in a very seductive voice, "— tend to your eye."

"Thanks, but my eye will be all right."

"Do I have to draw you a picture, Mr. MacCallister?" Kathleen said. "I don't intend that we use the double bed just for me to look after your eye."

Falcon shook his head. "Now, how would it look for you to run out on your own party like that?"

Kathleen looked taken aback that the offer to share her bed was rejected. Then she nodded.

"Yes, I suppose you are right," she said. "But remember, the offer is always open."

"I'll keep that in mind," Falcon said. He ameliorated his rejection with a smile. "I'd be a fool not to."

His smile and response soothed her hurt feelings, and she leaned over to kiss him on the cheek.

"Hey, Kathleen, how about a song?" someone shouted.

"Yeah, let's hear a song!"

Kathleen turned and walked back toward the piano. "Don't you boys get enough?" she asked, addressing everyone in the room. "I have already sung for two hours tonight."

"Just one more," someone pleaded.

"Yeah, just one more," another called.

Sylvester called over to her. "Come on, Kathleen. This is your party, after all. You'd better give them what they're asking for," he said.

"All right, boys," Kathleen agreed. "But if I wake up without a voice tomorrow, it'll be your fault."

Kathleen stepped over to the piano, then began looking through some music sheets. Finally, she selected one and handed it to the pianist.

"Play this one, Jimmy," she said. " 'My Darling Nellie Gray.' "

Jimmy played the first few bars of the introduction to the song, and then Kathleen began to sing.

There's a low green valley on the old
  Kentucky shore,

There I've whiled many happy hours
  away,
A-sitting and a-singing by the little
  cottage door
Where lived my darling Nelly Gray.
Oh! my poor Nelly Gray, they have taken
  you away,
  And I'll never see my darling anymore,
I'm sitting by the river and I'm weeping all
    the day,
  For you've gone from the old Kentucky
    shore.

Falcon slipped out of the saloon while Kathleen was still singing, then walked through the town until he reached the Martin house. He started to go around to the back entrance that led to his private room, but the front door opened and Frances stepped out onto the front porch.

"Mr. MacCallister, I'm still up," she said. "You can come in this way if you'd like."

"Thanks," Falcon said, stepping up onto the porch.

Frances moved back to let him in, then frowned as she saw his eye.

"Oh, my," she said, putting her fingers up to touch the red and black swelling. "What happened to your eye?"

Frances's fingers felt cool to the heated

swelling around his eye.

"I sort of ran into somebody's fist," Falcon replied with a chuckle.

"I hope the other fella looks worse," Frances said.

"I don't know how he could," Falcon said. "I haven't seen myself in a mirror yet, but I have a feeling this looks pretty bad."

"Come on into the parlor and sit down," Frances invited. "Let me see if I can do something about your eye."

"Ah, don't worry about it," Falcon said dismissively. "It'll be all right."

"Nonsense. I've seen wounds like this before. It will swell shut if you don't let me take care of it."

Falcon sat down in the parlor as Frances disappeared. She returned a moment later with a piece of raw, red steak.

"What are you doing?" Falcon asked, surprised to see the steak in her hand.

"There is nothing better than a piece of steak to keep the swelling down," Frances said.

"Yes, I've heard that. But Frances, I can't let you waste a good steak like that just to put over my eye. Not with the cost of meat."

Frances chuckled. "It's not actually a waste," she said. "This was supposed to be your steak, but you didn't eat dinner here tonight."

"No, I didn't," Falcon said quietly. He sighed. "But I should have," Falcon said. "It would have saved a lot of trouble."

"You mean like the shooting in the theater and down by the depot?"

"You've heard about that already?"

"Cody told me," Frances said. "He said he saw the whole thing. Or at least, he saw the part that happened at the depot."

"Yes, Cody was there," Falcon said. "I'm sorry that it happened at the depot. Especially as the train was coming in. I'm very lucky that it wasn't much worse than it was."

"From what Cody tells me, you didn't have any choice."

"That's true, but . . ." Falcon paused in mid-sentence.

"But what?"

"I never seem to have any choice when something like this happens," Falcon said. "But I must be responsible, because it happens so often. The average person doesn't suddenly find himself in a deadly shoot-out."

Inexplicably, and much to Falcon's surprise, Frances laughed out loud.

"What's so funny?" Falcon asked, curious at her strange reaction.

"Falcon MacCallister, what in the world

195

ever gave you the idea that you are an 'average' person? I've never met anyone who was less average than you," Frances said.

Falcon laughed as well. "I guess you've got me there," he said. "But then, you can hardly call yourself an average person either, any woman who can shoot as well as you do."

"Well, then, I suppose we are just two extraordinary people, aren't we?" Frances said. "Let me see how your steak is doing."

Frances leaned over Falcon to remove the piece of steak from his eye. He was exceptionally aware of the nearness of her lithe form, curved in all the right places, her shining hair, her large, wide-set eyes, and her high cheekbones. He could also smell a hint of lilac.

"Where is Gordon?" Falcon asked.

"He is spending the night with his cousin," Frances said, closing the distance between them.

Falcon felt her lips on his, and though he had resisted Kathleen's earlier advance, he did nothing to discourage Frances.

"Damn, Carney, you look half beat to death," Johnny Purvis said to his brother. "What happened?"

"It don't matter what happened," Carney

said. "I went into town like you said. And you're right, there is a lot of money in that town. I wouldn't be surprised if there wasn't more money in the bank there right now than in just about ever' other town in the West put together."

Johnny smiled and nodded. "I told you that. I've had someone on the inside from the first day."

"Yeah," Carney said. "I have to hand it to you, Johnny. You've had this all planned out from the beginning. You always was smarter'n me."

"It's not very hard to be smarter than you," Johnny said.

"Oh, now, Johnny, you got no call to say somethin' like that. Us bein' brothers an' all."

"We're half brothers," Johnny said. "We've got the same ma, that's all. Thank God we don't have the same pa."

"Well, that still don't give you no call to be callin' me dumb all the time."

"I thought I told you to just go into town and see if all the cattlemen had arrived yet."

"That's what I done."

"And I thought I told you to not call any attention to yourself."

"I didn't plan on callin' attention to myself," Carney answered.

"Carney, what in the hell did you expect when you got into a fight?" Johnny asked. "Hell, as big as you are, you call attention to yourself just by being there. But to start a fight, and lose the fight."

"How do you know I lost?" Carney asked.

"Come on, this is me you're talkin' to, remember. If you come slinkin' in here lookin' like you look now, that means you lost the fight. Now, who did you lose the fight to?"

"Falcon MacCallister," Carney said.

"Falcon MacCallister?" Johnny replied. "Are you crazy? What would make you pick a fight with Falcon MacCallister? Especially now, when we're trying to get this job set up?"

"Didn't you say he was the one that got you took to jail up in Miles City?" Carney asked.

"So what if I did? That's none of your concern," Johnny replied.

"Yeah, well, he had just kilt somebody," Carney said. "And ever'one was congratulatin' him, and makin' over him like he was some kind of a hero or somethin'. And I got to thinkin' about the run-in you had with him up in Miles City, so I figured I'd teach him a lesson."

"Yeah, it looks like you taught him a lesson, all right," Johnny said sarcastically.

The smell of brewing coffee awakened Falcon the next morning. He lay in bed for a moment, thinking about the night before. It had been good, better than good. Frances was not only a beautiful woman; it turned out that she was a surprisingly passionate woman as well.

Frances had not spent the entire night in his bed, and when he awoke this morning he wondered for a moment if it had actually happened. Had she really come to his bed, or had it just been a dream? No, it was no dream. She had shared his bed with him. He could still smell the hint of lilac on the pillow and in the sheets.

It had not been in Falcon's plans to have an affair with Frances, especially since she had a son to raise. Falcon did not have a history of butting into other people's families.

But Falcon was not the one who initiated it. It had been Frances. And when the beautiful, passionate woman launched her campaign to get Falcon in bed, he found it impossible to resist her charms.

Falcon swung his legs over and sat up on the edge of the bed. The first item of clothing he put on was his hat; then he reached for the rest of his clothes. Five minutes later he walked into the kitchen, where he saw Frances, standing over the wood-burning stove, fixing breakfast.

"I hope you like hotcakes," she said as she poured some of the beaten pancake batter into a big black iron skillet.

"I love hotcakes," Falcon answered.

"Good."

"Frances?"

"Yes?" Finished pouring the first cake, Frances rubbed the back of her hand on her face, leaving a small smear of flour on her forehead.

"About last night," Falcon began.

"Stop," Frances said, holding up her hand. Falcon grew quiet.

"I don't want you to get the wrong idea," Frances said. Holding the spatula in her right hand, she lifted her hand to rub her face, and she left another mark of flour on her forehead.

"The wrong idea?" Falcon replied.

"Yes, the wrong idea. I like you, Falcon. I like you a lot. But I have a responsibility to my son. What happened last night . . . what we did last night, has to stay right here. We can't carry it any further. I . . . I just can't get married again. I hope you understand."

Falcon nodded. "I understand," he said.

"Good. What we had between us last night was beautiful, like a flower that blooms and lives but one day. That is the way it is going to have to be with us, Falcon. We should never do this again. We can't ever do it again."

Falcon felt a sense of relief. He did not want to be involved with any woman. He was not in a position to be involved with any woman. He had made too many enemies and when his enemies came after him, they weren't all that discriminating. The experience with his wife, Mary, proved that. She was killed by men who wanted to kill him.

Even last night, the stagehand was killed simply because he had the misfortune of standing near where Falcon was sitting.

"You do understand, don't you?" Frances asked.

Falcon nodded. "I understand," he said.

Frances let out a big sigh of relief; then she smiled.

"I'm glad," she said. "Now, have a seat. The hotcakes will be ready soon."

From *The Sentinel:*

CITY CELEBRATION MARRED BY BRUTAL SLAYING!

Evening of Beautiful Music Ruined By A Madman.

GUNSHOTS FILLED THE STREET.
Slayer Is Himself Slain!
By JAMES HAYFORD, Publisher.

On Friday last, the citizens of our fair town were entertained by a young woman whose singing voice can only be compared to that of the angels, heralding some glad tidings from above. All left the theater imbued with the spirit of joy over having been witness to such beautiful singing as performed by Miss Kathleen Coyle.

But alas, our fair city was not long to relish this state of joy and contentment. Indeed, a scent of sulfur permeated the very air when a brigand by the name of Gilly Cardis, recently escaped from prison in Yuma, Arizona Territory, saw fit to bring evil upon us.

Brutally killing Paul Mobley, an innocent young man employed as a stagehand for the theater, Cardis then fled from the theater, being pursued by Deputy Seth Joyner and Mr. Falcon MacCallister, a visiting cattleman in town for the Hereford Auction, yet to be held.

Fleeing to the railroad station, Cardis used the coward's cover of darkness, surprised young Deputy Sheriff Seth Joyner by shooting him at point-blank range. His exchange of shots with Falcon MacCallister proved to be a fatal mistake on his part, however, for Mr. MacCallister dispatched him with but one shot from his pistol.

For the readers of this newspaper who are not familiar with Falcon MacCallister, he is a man known throughout the West for the quickness of his gun, the unerring accuracy of his eye, and his sense of justice, seeking always to right wrong and defend the defenseless.

FOURTEEN

Gabe Harland and Pete Ward started through the narrow draw that led through the south range of the Laramie Mountains and into a hidden valley. Suddenly, a rifle shot rang out. The bullet hit the sheer rock side of the wall, then ricocheted back with a loud singing whine that echoed and re-echoed throughout the length of the narrow pass.

"What the hell!" Pete shouted, pulling his horse back around the bend in the pass, and out of the line of fire. "Why are they shooting at us?"

"Wait a minute, Pete," Gabe called to the rider in front of him. "Don't go in there yet."

"Why not? This here is the place where we're supposed to meet 'em at, ain't it?"

"Don't you remember that Eddie Jordan give us these pieces of red cloth to put on our hat so's we can let 'em know who we are?"

"Oh," Pete said. "Yeah, I forgot."

"Uh-huh, an' forgettin' is what near 'bout got your ass shot off."

The two pulled the red cloths from their saddlebags, then, as instructed, stuck the cloths down into the headbands of their hats.

"Wait a minute," Gabe said.

"Wait for what?"

Gabe took the red cloth off his hat and tied it on the end of his rifle.

"What are you doin' that for?"

"I think we'd better let 'em know about the red cloth before we go in again," Gabe said.

Dismounted, he walked up to the turn in the narrow draw, then stuck the rifle out around the corner and waved it up and down several times.

"You think that'll do it?" Pete asked.

"I don't know," Gabe said. "I hope so. Ride on in now, real slow."

"Me ride in? Why should I ride in?"

" 'Cause you're the one that got us into this predicament in the first place," Gabe said. "You're the one who rode in without so much as a fare-thee-well and with no red in your hat."

Pete paused for a moment. "All right, I'll ride in. But you stay out of my way because if they shoot again, I'm hightailin' it out of there."

"Hold your hands up as you ride in. Maybe if they see that, they'll see that we're comin' as friends."

With the piece of red cloth prominently displayed on his hat, Pete rode back around the corner of the draw with his hands held up.

"All right," Pete said. "They ain't a'shootin' this time. Come on, let's go on in."

Cautiously, Gabe put the red cloth back into his hatband and came into the draw behind Pete. They urged their mounts ahead and the horses picked their way through the narrow draw, the hoof falls on the rocky floor echoing back from the encroaching walls.

"Hey, Gabe, you got you sort of a prickly feelin' on the back of your neck? Like we're bein' watched?" Pete asked.

" 'Course we're bein' watched," Gabe replied.

As they got closer, someone suddenly appeared, standing on top of a large overhang ahead of them. He was holding a rifle as he stared down at them.

Because Pete was still leading the way, he was the only one of the two to see him.

"Hold it, Gabe," Pete said. "Take a look up there."

Looking up, Gabe saw the man watching them. Gabe made a big show of taking off his hat, and pointing to the splash of red in his hatband. The man on the rock held out his hand as if to stop them, then pulled his pistol.

"What the hell is he a'doin'?" Pete asked.

"Wait," Gabe said. "Don't move or do nothin' till he tells us to."

The man on the rock fired his pistol into the air, two shots, a pause, then a third shot.

After the echoes of his shooting died, there came back an answering signal, the rhythmic patter just the opposite of the first signal. This time it was one shot, a pause, and then two shots.

The man on the rock waved his hand, motioning for them to come on in.

The entrance to the hidden valley was long and twisting, and in places so narrow that it barely afforded enough space for one horse and rider to squeeze through. When they finally emerged at the other end, they were met by Eddie Jordan, the man who had not only given them the red cloth, but had provided them with the directions on how to get there.

"Hello, Eddie," Gabe said.

"Hello, Gabe, Pete," Eddie Jordon replied. "Did you have any trouble finding the place?"

"No. But I'm glad you told us about the red cloth. Otherwise, we might be lyin' belly-down back in the draw."

"No 'might be' to it," another man said, coming up to greet them then. "You would be dead."

"Who are you?" Gabe asked.

"This here is Poke," Eddie said.

"Poke?"

"You got a problem with that name?" Poke asked.

"No, I don't have a problem," Gabe said.

"Poke here will take you to meet the boss," Eddie said.

"Why can't you take us?"

"I got you in here," Eddie said. "I don't need to hold your hand."

As Gabe and Pete followed Poke, they looked around. There had evidently been a homestead here at one time and some of the original buildings remained. A large red barn, badly faded from years of exposure to the weather, was the biggest building noticeable. There was also a two-story house near the barn, part of the original homestead. In addition, there were a few buildings constructed of shale rock and mud, a few more made of twigs and mud, and at least half-a-dozen tents and a few lean-tos. One enterprising soul had constructed a hasty saloon by stretching a plank across two empty barrels. A handful of men were standing by the makeshift bar, availing themselves of the services.

A short distance away from the improvised saloon, four men were tossing horseshoes. The clank of one of the tossed shoes elicited groans from two of them, and cheers from the other two. At still another location a few men were sitting by a fire, cooking something, while at various other locations in the camp men were engaged in activities from playing mumblety-peg to just talking. And to Gabe and Pete's surprise, they saw a few women as well.

"What is this place?" Pete asked. "Damn me if this don't almost look like a town."

"Well, it's sort of like a town. We call it Last Chance," Poke said.

"But is it a real town? I mean, I see that some of the men have their wives here. Funny, though, I don't see no kids."

"You don't see no kids 'cause there ain't no kids. Them women ain't wives. They're whores," Poke said.

"Is there a sheriff, or anything like that?"

"Ain't got a sheriff, and I don't figure this would be too hospitable a place for a sheriff."

When they reached the original house, still the most substantial of all the buildings, Poke pointed to a hitching rail in front of the house.

"You can tie your horses up here until you've had your meeting."

"What meeting?" Gabe asked.

"Johnny likes to meet with ever'body when they first come into Last Chance."

"Johnny who?"

"Johnny Purvis. This is his house," Poke said.

"This looks a lot like a ranch," Gabe said. "Did Johnny build it?"

Poke laughed. "Johnny don't build nothin'," he said. "He just takes whatever he wants or needs."

"What happened to the people who built it?"

"Damn, you ask a lot of questions, don't you?" Poke said. "This ain't a place where we ask questions."

"Ain't he goin' to ask us some questions?" Pete asked.

"Yeah, but that's different."

"What's different about it?"

"You don't think he's going to just let anybody ride in here, do you?"

"What should we tell him?"

"How the hell do I know what to tell him?" Poke replied. "Look, I'm just pointin' out the house to you two boys. I sure as hell didn't take you to raise."

Gabe and Pete watched as Poke left; then they walked up the little rocky path that led to the house and knocked on the door.

"Yeah, come in!" a muffled voice replied.

Gabe opened the door and the two of them stepped inside. They saw a big man sitting at the table, eating beans.

"Who are you?" the big man asked, looking up as Gabe and Pete came into the room.

"My name's Gabe Harland, Mr. Purvis. This here is Pete Ward."

"I ain't Johnny," the big man said.

"I thought this was Mr. Purvis's house," Gabe said.

"It is his house. I'm his brother, Carney. Johnny's out back, takin' a piss."

At that moment the back door opened and a man came in. He was tall, with dark eyes and a black, sweeping mustache. He had a dark, very visible scar on his left cheek.

"Are you Johnny?" Gabe asked.

"I'll ask the questions here," the man

replied. "Who are you?" He stroked the scar on his cheek.

"Oh. Uh, well, I'm Gabe Harland and this is Pete Ward. If you're Johnny, we was told to tell you that Eddie Jordan talked to you about us. I don't know if you remember or anything."

"I remember," Johnny said.

Gabe waited for him to say something else, and when the pregnant pause grew uncomfortably long, he cleared his throat and spoke again.

"The thing is . . . I thought . . . well, that is, Eddie said, you might have some kind of job for us."

"That depends," Johnny replied.

"Depends on what?"

"On whether or not you can follow orders."

"Who's givin' the orders?" Gabe asked.

"I give the orders," Johnny said. "Do you have any trouble with that?"

Gabe and Pete looked at each other for a moment before Gabe answered. "I ain't got no problem with takin' orders," he said.

"How about you?" Johnny asked Pete. "Do you have any problem with takin' orders?"

Pete shook his head. "No," he said. "I ain't got a problem with that."

Johnny nodded. "Good. You follow instructions and we'll get along just fine. And you'll make yourselves a lot of money."

Both Gabe and Pete smiled.

"We're all for makin' money," Pete said.

"How are we goin' to do it?" asked Gabe.

"I'm goin' to have a meetin' this afternoon," Johnny said. "You show up for that meeting and you'll find out ever'thing you need to know."

"We'll be there," Gabe said.

"Good," Johnny said.

"Johnny, they's some beans there in the can if you're hungry," Carney said.

"Thanks."

Johnny picked up the can and began eating beans, but when he noticed that neither Gabe nor Pete left, he stopped eating and looked up at them. "Why are you still here?" he asked.

Pete and Gabe looked at each other, then, by silent agreement, Gabe spoke for both of them.

"Speakin' of tonight," he said. "Where are me and Pete supposed to sleep?"

"Where'd you sleep last night?" Johnny asked, shoveling a spoonful of beans into his mouth.

"We just throw'd us out a bedroll on the trail," Pete said.

Johnny nodded. "Sounds like a good enough plan to me."

When the two men went outside, they saw Eddie waiting for them.

"What do you think?" Eddie asked.

"Think about what? He didn't tell us nothin'," Gabe said.

"Except we're goin' to have a meeting this afternoon."

"Yeah," Eddie said. "Accordin' to what I hear, he's got a job planned that's so big it's goin' to make us rich."

Pete shook his head. "I don't know. I count at least a dozen men here. It's goin' to take an awful lot of money to make all of us rich."

"This is sort of an outlaws' roost," Eddie said. "Which means that ever' one here is wanted by the law for one thing or another. But it don't mean that ever' one here is goin' to be a part of what Johnny is cookin' up. But the ones that is, is goin' to make a lot of money. Or so they say."

"Who is 'they'?" Gabe asked.

"They," Eddie said without further explanation.

That same afternoon, just after lunch, Gabe, Pete, Eddie, Poke, Carney, and several others, though not all of the men in camp, were gathered around the front of Johnny's cabin. Johnny stepped outside and looked at all of them for a moment, then nodded.

"Boys, I'm about to tell you what I've got planned," he said. "If you ain't interested, walk away now."

"Is there shootin' involved?" one of the men asked.

"There might be," Johnny said.

"Then I ain't interested."

"All right. Ain't nobody sayin' you got to come," Johnny said. "Anybody else not interested?"

"Is it true, like they're saying, that there's a lot of money to be made?" another man asked.

"That's true," Johnny said.

"Look here, Johnny, whatever you got planned, it ain't goin' to bring the law down on us in here, is it?" one of the others asked. "We got us a good thing in here."

"Don't you be worryin' about it, Quincy. It ain't goin' to bring the law in here," Johnny said. "Now, are you staying or walkin' away? I only want men I can count on."

"I'm walkin' away," Quincy said. "Any of you comin' with me?"

Quincy looked at all the others, and while

215

a few shifted their weight nervously from foot to foot, none of them joined him.

"Fine," Quincy said. "I wish you fellas good luck, but count me out."

Johnny nodded, then waited until Quincy was out of hearing range.

"All right," he said. "From this point on, you are all in on the deal."

"What is the deal?" Gabe asked.

"Maybe some of you boys don't know what's goin' on in Laramie right now," Johnny said. "So I'm going to tell you. There is going to be a special auction take place in a few days, where several head of the best blooded Hereford cattle will be sold."

"That's it?" one of the men said. "We're going to steal cows? To hell with that. If I wanted to be a cowboy, I'd still be riding for twelve dollars a month and found."

"We aren't going to be stealing cows," Johnny said. "What we are going to steal is the money that has been brought into town to buy these cows."

"How much money will that be?"

"Conrad Kohrs will be there," Johnny said. "Also Shanghai Pierce, Alexander Swan, and John Wesley Iliff, just to name a few. I figure, all told, there will be at least fifty of the richest cattlemen in the country there, and they'll probably bring about ten thousand dollars apiece to have ready for the auction. That's half a million dollars," he said.

The response from the men was instantaneous as they began babbling in excitement. Johnny held up his hands to call for quiet. "As you can see," he said, "that is plenty enough money for all of us."

"What's the plan?" Pete asked.

"I'll let the rest of you in on the plan as soon as I think you need to know," he said.

"How do you know all these people you said are there?" Gabe asked.

"Because I have someone in town, keeping me up on what's going on. When it's time to make our move, I'll know, then I'll tell you. In the meantime, make sure your horses are healthy and your guns are in good working order. You have to be ready to go the moment I give you the word."

"Hey, Johnny, I count ten of us here," one of the men said. "So, what you're sayin' is, we'll be getting fifty thousand dollars apiece?"

Johnny shook his head. "It won't be ten people dividing half a million dollars. It'll be nine people dividing a quarter of a million."

"How do you figure that?"

"I figure that because I'm takin' half of

whatever we get for myself."

"The hell you say. If you take half of the money, I don't want no part of it."

Johnny pulled his pistol and pointed it at the protester. He cocked the hammer.

"It's too late," Johnny said. "You might remember I told you that if you wanted no part of it, you should leave. Now, you can't leave, so you have a choice. You can take your share of a quarter of a million dollars, or you can die."

"Don't be a fool, Metz," one of the others said to the man who was protesting. "Your share of a quarter of a million will come to over twenty-five thousand dollars."

"Twenty-five thousand?" Metz asked. The expression of fear on his face was replaced by a wide grin. "Oh, well, hell, why didn't you say so? Count me in."

Johnny continued to hold the gun pointed at Metz for a long moment, the hammer held back by his thumb. He held it for so long that the smile on Metz's face disappeared to be replaced, once again, by an expression of fear.

Finally, Johnny eased the hammer down, and put his pistol back in his holster. "I'll not be questioned again, by anyone," he said. "Do I make myself clear?"

There was dead silence from the men.

"Do I make myself clear?" he asked again, this time in clipped words that demanded a response.

"Yes," the men all answered as one.

"Good. Now we understand each other."

Johnny went back into his cabin and the others drifted away singly, or in pairs, or small groups. After a moment of contemplation over how close they'd come to seeing one of their number killed, they began thinking of how much money each of them might make, and as a result, began talking about it in excited voices.

"You think Johnny would have killed Metz?" Pete asked.

"Yeah," Poke said. "He would have killed him."

"I don't mind tellin' you, Johnny ain't the kind of man I feel easy about ridin' for," Pete said. "What do you think, Gabe?"

"What do I think?" Gabe replied. "I think that, for the kind of money we're talking about, I'd soak my pants in coal oil and ride for the devil himself."

Fifteen

"Is that what we're buying?" Shanghai Pierce asked. Falcon MacCallister, Alexander Swan, Shanghai Pierce, George Littlefield, Conrad Kohrs, and several other cattlemen were down at the holding pens to get a look at the Herefords.

"That's what we are buying, gentlemen," Kohrs replied. "Purebred Hereford cattle."

"I'll say this for them, they are a lot bigger than a longhorn," Pierce said. "What do you think about them, George?"

"Gentlemen," Littlefield replied. "The only practical knowledge I have gained in my ranching experience is to be able to say, with certainty, that a cow will have a calf."

The others laughed.

"Are they going to cost us a lot more to raise?" Swan asked.

"No," Kohrs said, shaking his head. "That is the great beauty of raising Herefords. Gentlemen, it will cost us about the same amount of money to raise a Hereford as it does to raise a longhorn, but we will get at least three times as much money per animal. Think about it. You can increase your profit by three hundred percent just by changing breeds."

As the cattlemen continued to examine the Herefords, Kohrs came over to talk to Falcon. Falcon was leaning on the fence, looking just over the top at the cows.

"What do you think of them?" Kohrs asked.

"You had me convinced back in Miles City," Falcon said. "When the auction starts, I'll be bidding."

Kohrs chuckled. "I may have done too good a job in selling the concept," he said. "So many people are going to be bidding on the cows now that it's going to run the price up."

"I'm sure you can afford it," Falcon said.

Kohrs laughed, then took in the other cattlemen with a sweep of his hand. "So can they," he said. "And that's the problem. We can all afford it."

"Yes, and here I am, a lamb come to the slaughter," Falcon said. "I feel out of place with all the big boys here."

"Ha!" Kohrs said. "You probably take more money out of one of your gold or silver mines than we generate with all our ranches combined."

"Well, I am coming to the auction," Falcon said.

"A lamb to the slaughter?" Kohrs teased.

"Maybe not quite that bad," Falcon admitted.

"If I haven't said it before, Falcon, I'm glad you are participating," Kohrs said. "A lot of people respect you. When it gets out that you are running Herefords, it will do a lot for the cattle industry."

"I'm keeping some of my longhorns, though," Falcon said.

"Oh, I'm sure we all are," Kohrs said. "I confess to having some affection for the creatures."

"Mr. MacCallister?" someone said, and Falcon turned to see a balding man of small stature standing nearby. It was easy to see that he was balding because he was holding his hat in his hand.

"Yes?" Falcon asked.

"My name is Reavis. Glen Reavis," the balding man said.

"What can I do for you, Mr. Reavis?"

"I was wondering if you would sign this for me," said Reavis. "Sort of an autograph, so to speak."

Reavis held something out toward Falcon.

Taking it, Falcon saw that it was a photograph of the corpse of Gilly Cardis.

"What the hell is this?" Falcon asked sharply, handing the picture back.

"It's a photo of the man you kilt yesterday," Reavis said.

"Where did you get such a thing?"

"From Dysart's photo shop," Reavis said. "He took a picture of the corpse and he's sellin' photographs for fifty cents the picture."

"And people are actually buying them?" Falcon asked.

"Yes, sir. They're goin' like hotcakes," Reavis said. "Uh . . . will you sign my picture?"

Falcon shook his head. "No," he said. "I'm not going to autograph the picture of a man I killed."

"It'd make a fine keepsake," Reavis said.

"Go away, Mr. Reavis," Kohrs said. "You heard the man. He's not going to sign it."

Reavis stood for a moment longer, then nodded and left.

"Anything like that ever happened to you before?" Kohrs asked.

"You mean has anyone ever asked me to sign the photograph of someone I killed? No, it hasn't. And I hope it never happens again."

Suddenly Kohrs chuckled.

"What's so funny?"

"I bet I know something else that's never happened to you before, and that you hope doesn't happen again."

"What's that?"

"You losin' a shootin' match to a woman," Kohrs said. "Or at least, almost losing to a woman."

Falcon smiled and nodded. "That's true," he said. "She matched me shot for shot. In the end, I only beat her on time, not on shooting."

"Who is she? I know you people who are really good with a gun keep up on each other. Had you ever heard of her before? Do you know her?"

"No, I'd never heard of her. And I didn't know her until I came to Laramie," Falcon said. "But I know her now. Her name is Frances Martin, and she runs a boardinghouse."

"A boardinghouse, you say?"

"A small boardinghouse," Falcon said. "In fact, I'm staying there while I'm in town."

"You don't say?" Kohrs replied. "I didn't see the shooting match, but I heard she was quite a looker. Anything to that?"

"She is a very pretty woman," Falcon agreed.

"A pretty woman and a good shot. I'll bet you have some interesting conversations around the dinner table."

"Would you like another serving of pot roast, Mr. MacCallister?" Frances asked.

Falcon smiled. Frances was going out of her way to be formal and precise today, probably because Gordon was at the table. Falcon could understand her reasoning, but he found it humorous, when contrasting it with the passionate woman she was last night.

"No, thank you, Mrs. Martin," he said, rubbing his stomach. "Everything is so delicious that I'm afraid I ate too much. If I eat any more I might just pop open."

"Oh, that's too bad," Frances said. "I should have told you to save some room for some sweet-potato pie."

"Sweet-potato pie?" Falcon said, brightening. "Well, I suppose I can find room for that."

Frances laughed. "I was hoping you could," she said.

"Mr. MacCallister, would you tell me what it is like?" Gordon asked.

"What what is like?"

"Yesterday, when you killed that bad man. What was it like?"

"Gordon!" Frances said sharply. "How could you ask such a thing?"

"I just want to know what it's like, Mom, that's all," Gordon said. "I've read about him in the stories. In the stories he always says, 'Get ready to eat your supper in hell.' Did you say that to him?"

"Gordon, apologize to Mr. MacCallister," Frances said. "You apologize right now, young man."

"No, wait," Falcon said, lifting his hand. He looked at Gordon for a long moment, then sighed, and ran his hand across his mouth. "It's not like that, Gordon," he said.

"What do you mean?"

"In the first place, I have never told anyone to get ready to eat supper in hell."

"But all the stories I've read . . ."

"Are wrong," Falcon said before Gordon could finish. "You want to know what it's like to kill a man?"

"Yes!" Gordon said excitedly.

"It's like sticking your fingers so far down your throat that you want to throw up," Falcon said.

"What?"

"The man I shot yesterday woke up just like I did, just like everyone else did. He thought this would just be another day like every other day in his life. But it wasn't. It was the last day of his life, because I took his life away from him.

"He may have been an evil man yesterday, when I shot him. But you know that he wasn't always evil. He was a kid once, playing games like other kids. All those memories he had, of the games he played, the friends he had, the family he knew, are gone now, and I took them away from him.

"No, Gordon, it's not glorious, it's not thrilling. It's not a good feeling at all. It's sort of a sick feeling."

"Then why do you do it?"

"It's not something I do by choice," Falcon said. "And believe me, if I could walk away from this and never do it again, I would."

"I . . . I guess I never thought about it like that," Gordon said. "Mom?"

Inexplicably, there were tears in Frances's eyes.

"Mom, why are you crying?"

Frances wiped her eyes with the hem of her apron. "I was moved by Mr. MacCallister's words," she said. She forced a smile. "Well, are you ready for your pie?"

"Can I have my pie later?" Gordon asked. "I don't really feel like eating it right now. I think I'll go to my room."

"All right," Frances said. "Whenever you

feel ready for your pie, you can just come get a piece."

"Thanks. And Mr. MacCallister, if I don't see you again today, good night."

"Good night, Gordon."

Frances cut a generous piece of pie and put it on Falcon's plate.

"Thanks," Falcon said.

"And thank you for talking to Gordon like that," Frances said. "I wasn't sure where that conversation was leading, but I see now, and I think you did a good thing."

"Don't be hard on him, Frances," Falcon said, using her first name now that Gordon was out of earshot. "Kids his age have a fascination with such things."

"I know. That's why I have held off teaching him to shoot."

Falcon shook his head. "No, don't do that," he said. "He needs to know how to shoot, as much for his confidence and self-esteem as anything else." He smiled. "And it would be a shame for you not to pass on to him the skills you learned from your father."

"I guess you're right," Frances said.

"Uhmm," Falcon said as he took his first bite. "This has to be about the best pie I have ever tasted. Frances, you not only shoot well, you are a culinary genius."

Frances smiled coquettishly. "Falcon MacCallister, if you ever think about me in the future, I hope that you remember more than my shooting and cooking skills."

"Don't worry about that," Falcon said in a low, husky voice. "You've given me ample reason to remember you for far more than that."

Frances sighed, and looked toward Gordon's room. "Unfortunately, memory is all we will have," she said.

Sixteen

Johnny Purvis held up his hand to signal a stop, and the nine riders who were with him hauled back on their reins.

A few of the others spoke to their animals as they stopped them.

"Whoa!"

"Hold it."

"Come back."

Johnny took his canteen from the saddle pommel and took a drink, then offered it to his brother.

Carney took a swallow, then spit it out. "Damn!" he said. "That's water."

"Yes."

"What the hell did you offer me a drink of water for? If I wanted water, I'd drink from my own canteen."

"Would you now?" Johnny asked. He held his hand out. "Let me have a drink."

"What do you mean? You've got your own water," Carney said.

"Let me have a drink," Johnny said again.

Reluctantly, Carney handed his canteen over to Johnny. Johnny pulled the cork, sniffed it, then took a drink. He spit it out immediately.

"Just as I thought," he said. "Whiskey." Johnny turned the canteen upside down and began pouring out the whiskey.

"Johnny, what are you doing?" Carney asked with a pained expression in his voice.

"I'm pouring out your whiskey," he said. He turned in his saddle to address the other riders. "All of you," he said. "If any of you have whiskey, pour it out now."

Nobody moved.

"Get your canteens up, and pull the cork," he said. "I'm going to check every one. If you've got whiskey, I'm going to pour it out."

"You got no right to pour out my whiskey," one of the riders said.

"You can keep your whiskey if you want to, Snyder," Johnny said.

"All right," Synder said with a broad smile.

"But if you keep it, you have to go back."

"What?" Snyder asked.

Johnny pointed back down the trail. "If your whiskey is more important than the money you'll be getting from this job, go on

231

back," he said. "I don't intend to have any drunks with me when we pull this off."

Snyder glared at Johnny for a moment; then he began emptying his canteen. The others emptied their canteens as well. Only Eddie Jordan, Gabe Harland, and Pete Ward did not.

"You boys have only water?" Johnny asked.

"Yeah, Johnny, I told 'em you wouldn't want no drinkin'," Eddie said.

Johnny nodded. "Good man," he said.

"How much farther is it?" Carney asked.

Johnny pulled out his watch and looked at it. "It's eleven o'clock now," he said. "We'll be there about two."

"What about eatin'?" Poke asked. "Are we goin' to eat?"

"You got jerky, don't you?"

"Yeah."

"Eat in your saddle."

"Jerky ain't no good if you don't have somethin' to wash it down with."

"It's not my fault you don't have water," Johnny said. "Let's get goin'."

Falcon was standing at the bar in the Gold Strike Saloon. There were only four others in the saloon at the moment, and Falcon looked at the Regulator Clock sitting near the piano at the back of the room. It was nearly two.

"Sort of quiet, isn't it?" Falcon asked.

"Always is this time of day," Sylvester said. Sylvester was busy behind the bar, counting money.

"Looks like you had a good day yesterday," Falcon said.

"I wish this was from one day," Sylvester said with a dry chuckle. "But I only make a deposit once a week and this is it."

Sylvester put the last of the money in a cloth bag, then called to Kathleen, who was sitting at a table near the piano, looking at sheet music.

"Kathleen, would you run this down to the bank for me?"

"Sure thing, Sylvester," Kathleen said, coming over to the bar.

"I'll go with you," Falcon offered.

"You don't need to," Kathleen said. "I can handle it by myself."

Falcon smiled. "The way you talk, you'd think you don't want my company."

"No, it's not that," Kathleen said.

"I'm going to the bank anyway," he said. "I'm going to make arrangements to make a wire transfer of some more money. This auction might cost more than I thought and I want to make certain I have enough cash on hand to participate."

"All right," Kathleen said. "And of course I welcome your company, anytime . . . anywhere," she added, making the last word an invitation.

Falcon tossed down the last swallow of his beer, then walked to the batwing doors and held one of them open for her.

"Fire!" someone called. He was running up the middle of the street, yelling at the top of his lungs. "Fire! The feed store is on fire!"

Even as he was shouting the news, the blacksmith was ringing the fire alarm by banging his hammer against an iron ring. The church bell was ringing as well.

The fire had already gotten a good start in the feed store and a heavy column of smoke was climbing into the sky, while fingers of fire licked up along the side of the building.

Falcon and Kathleen stood beside the street for a minute, watching all the activity.

"Do you want to go down and watch it?" Kathleen said. "I can make the deposit myself." She smiled. "I know how all little boys enjoy a fire, and I believe that all men are little boys at heart."

Falcon chuckled. "No," he said. "I'd just get in the way."

"Make way! Make way!" someone was

shouting through a megaphone. Falcon looked around to see the fire engine being drawn at a gallop by a matched pair of white horses. Smoke was coming from the steam-powered pump, and one of the firemen was riding alongside the pumper, alternately shouting through a megaphone and blowing a bugle to warn people out of the way.

When they reached the bank, Falcon held the door open for Kathleen, and they stepped inside. There were no customers, but two men were standing at the front window of the bank, looking down toward the fire. Falcon had been in town long enough to have met both men, when he opened an account to use for the upcoming auction. One was Gene Frazier, the owner of the bank, and the other was Claude Mitchum, the teller.

"That's Mr. Dunnaway's place that's on fire," Mitchum said. "He and his family live in the back. I hope his wife and children got out safely."

"Even if they did, it is going to be difficult for them," Frazier said. "Dunnaway put everything he had into that store. I know because he had to borrow money from the bank to do it."

The two men looked around when they

heard Falcon and Kathleen come into the bank.

"Good morning," Falcon said.

"Good morning, Mr. MacCallister, Miss Coyle," Frazier said.

"That's quite a fire going on down there," Falcon said.

"Indeed it is. It seems to have drawn the entire town down to watch it. I didn't expect we would have any customers with the fire going on. What can we do for you?"

"Well, Miss Coyle has come to make a deposit for the Gold Strike," Falcon said. "And I want to arrange for a wire transfer of additional funds from my bank back in Colorado."

"Yes, sir," Frazier replied, smiling. "It's a pleasure to do business with one of our visiting cattle barons. Mr. Mitchum, would you take care of Miss Coyle, while I deal with Mr. MacCallister?"

"Yes, sir," Mitchum said.

Falcon chuckled. "I've never really thought of myself as a cattle baron."

"Perhaps not a baron in the sense that Kohrs and some of the others are," Mitchum agreed. "But from what I know of you, you are certainly stout enough to have a seat at their table. Now, how much money do you want to . . . ?"

At that moment, six masked men suddenly came rushing into the bank. All six had their guns drawn.

"What's going on here?" Frazier asked.

"Well, now, what does it look like?" one of the masked men said. "We have come to do a little business with you."

"What kind of business do you expect to do wearing masks like that?"

"Banking business," the man who seemed to be in charge said. "We are going to be making a withdrawal this morning." He laughed at his own joke.

Falcon had the feeling that he had met the laughing bank robber somewhere before, because there was something familiar about his voice. He knew that he had met one of the other bank robbers before, because he was considerably bigger than all the others. This was the man Falcon had had the fight with in the saloon.

"Hello, Carney," Falcon said.

"Johnny, he knows who I am!" Carney said.

Hearing the other man referred to as Johnny, Falcon knew who he was too, because now he knew where he had heard the voice.

"Johnny Purvis. I thought you were in jail up in Miles City," Falcon said in an open, friendly tone. "Gone into the bank-robbing business, have you?"

"You know what, MacCallister? You talk too much," Johnny said. He made a motion with his hand. "Take your pistol out of your holster."

Falcon reached for his gun.

"No, wait," Johnny said. "Girly, you do it. Do it slow and easy like," Johnny said. "Just use your thumb and one finger, and drop it into that spittoon over there."

Kathleen just stood there. "Don't make me do this," she said.

"Just do it, Girly."

Reluctantly, Kathleen did as she was told.

Carney pulled his mask off.

"What'd you do that for?" Johnny asked.

"Hell, Johnny, he knows who we are. And this mask itches."

"You're right," Johnny said. He took his mask off as well; then, as he fingered his scar, he smiled and looked at Falcon.

"You know who this is, don't you, boys?" Johnny said to the others. "This here is the great Falcon MacCallister. Some say he is the best gunfighter there ever was. But look at where his gun is now."

Looking at the spittoon, the masked outlaws all laughed.

"The fire down the street, the one that is

causing all the commotion," Falcon said. "You started it, didn't you?"

Johnny chuckled. "Well, now, maybe you ain't quite as dumb as you look. Yeah, I set the fire. I figured it would draw the whole town down there, and it did. And I've got men posted all up and down the street, so if anyone gets curious about what's goin' on here at the bank, and comes down to have a look-see, they'll be shot."

"Yeah," Carney said. "They'll be shot."

"You," Johnny said, handing a large canvas bag to Mitchum. "Start fillin' up this sack with money."

Nervously, Mitchum began scooping money out of the drawers. He dropped the money into the sack, then handed it back to Johnny.

Johnny looked down into the bag. "What the hell?" he said, sputtering. "What are you trying to pull here? This can't be much more'n a few thousand dollars."

"There are six thousand, two hundred, and forty-seven dollars in the bag," Mitchum said.

"Get the rest of it."

"That's all of it," Frazier said.

"Who are you?" Johnny demanded.

"My name is Gene Frazier. I own the bank."

"Well, Mr. Gene Frazier, I don't believe that's all of it," Johnny said. "You've got lots of rich men in this town now, to buy cattle. Are you tellin' me they haven't opened accounts here?"

"Yes, they have," Frazier replied.

"Then give me their money," Johnny demanded.

"You don't understand. They are all wire accounts. The money isn't here yet."

"They are what?"

"They are wire accounts," Frazier repeated.

"What does that mean?"

"It means that their actual money is back in their hometowns, in their own banks. There won't be any money put in this bank until their home bank is notified by telegram; then the money will be transferred here in time for the auction."

"What kind of fools do you take us for?" Johnny asked. "I don't know much about telegrams and the like, but I know for a fact that you can't send no money over a telegraph wire."

"It is an accounting transfer only," Frazier explained. "That will allow the cattlemen to write drafts against an account which will be paid when the money has been physically moved to this bank."

"What's this about, Johnny?" one of the other bank robbers asked angrily. "You told us the bank would be filled with money."

"Take it easy, Poke," Johnny said. "How the hell was I supposed to know about something called a wire transfer?" Johnny replied.

While the robbers were arguing among themselves, Gene Frazier suddenly grabbed a gun from a counter behind the teller window. He raised it to shoot, but was awkward with it, and the robbers, almost as one, turned their guns toward him and fired. Frazier went down, bleeding from multiple gunshot wounds.

"Damn!" Johnny said. "What did the son of a bitch do that for?"

"Come on, Johnny," Carney shouted. "We've got to get out of here!"

From outside could be heard more gunshots, and Snyder stuck his head in the through the front door.

"We've got to get out of here, boys!" he called. "They heard the shots and some folks are coming this way! We're keepin' 'em back, but there's only four of us."

"Let's go," Johnny said, and he and the other five men backed out of the bank with their guns pointed toward Falcon and Mitchum.

As soon as the bank robbers left, Falcon reached down into the spittoon and, disregarding the odorous brown ooze that was clinging to his gun, and now to his hand, rushed out the back door of the bank, then ran up the side of the bank building until he reached the street.

Falcon began shooting at the fleeing robbers. He killed one, and wounded another, knocking him from his horse, but the remaining eight managed to get away.

Sheriff Gibson and several other townspeople who were down by the fire had been alerted by the sound of gunshots coming from the bank. When they had started up the street toward the bank, however, they were fired upon by the four men Johnny had left out in the street. Now, with all the robbers in retreat, they came running up to the bank.

"The bank?" Sheriff Gibson asked as he came over to Falcon.

"Yes," Falcon answered.

Gibson nodded. "Yeah, I thought so. How many were there?"

"Ten, I think."

"Ten? Damn, that's a small army."

"There's two less now," one of the townspeople said. "There are two of them down."

"Sheriff, this one is still alive!" one of the

townspeople yelled.

"Get him down to the jail."

"He needs a doctor."

"Get him to the jail first, then get him a doctor," Sheriff Gibson said. Then to Falcon: "Was there anyone hurt in the bank?"

"They shot Frazier," Falcon said.

"How bad?"

"I think he's dead."

SEVENTEEN

Several of the townspeople got the wounded man to his feet, not too gently, and they brought him to the sheriff. He was holding his hand over a wound in his shoulder.

"Does anybody know this man?" Gibson asked.

"His name is Carney," someone said.

"Yeah, Carney," one of the others said. "You know him, don't you, MacCallister? You beat the hell out of him the other day."

"Yeah, I know him."

Gibson chuckled. "I heard about that fight. This is the one, huh?"

"Yes."

"Carney," Gibson said. "Is that your last name, or your first name?"

"It's my name," Carney said.

Sheriff Gibson shrugged. "All right, that's good enough for me. After we hang you, we'll just put Carney on your grave marker."

Carney shook his head and smiled. "My

brother ain't goin' to let you hang me," he said.

"We'll just see about that," Gibson said. "Get him out of here," he said, and as the townspeople took Carney down the street to the jail, Gibson and Falcon started back into the bank. Falcon stopped at a watering trough in front of the leather goods store next to the bank, and dunked his hand and gun down into the water. Then, his gun and hand clean, he followed the sheriff inside.

Mitchum was sitting on the floor with Frazier. Kathleen was standing over by one of the tables, looking away from the body.

"Is he dead?" Gibson asked.

Mitchum nodded, then replied in a choked voice, "Yes."

"I don't suppose you recognized any of them, did you?"

"I didn't actually recognize any of them," Mitchum said, "but they called one of them Johnny. Johnny Purvis."

"It was Johnny all right," Falcon said.

"You know Johnny?"

"I know him," said Falcon. "So does Miss Coyle."

"You know him, Miss Coyle?"

"No," Kathleen said quickly. "I don't know him."

"I didn't mean to say that you actually

know him," Falcon said. "I just meant that you met him, we both met him, up in Miles City."

"Oh," Kathleen said. "Oh, well, that may be. Though, I'm not sure that was the same person."

"You do remember him, don't you? He broke into your room. How could you forget him?"

"I just wanted to put that incident out of my mind. I was pretty upset the night that man broke into my room," Kathleen said. She nodded. "But now that you remind me of it, yes. Yes, I'm pretty sure that this was the same one."

"And his name is Johnny Purvis?" Gibson asked.

Kathleen nodded again. "Yes, that's what he said his name was."

"All right," Gibson said. "At least we have one name to go on."

When they reached a stream of water, the bank robbers stopped to water their horses.

"Six thousand dollars, huh?" one of the riders said. "That's a hell of a long way from half a million dollars."

"Yeah? Well, how much money did you have when you woke up this morning?" Johnny asked.

"About ten dollars."

"Well, now you have over four hundred dollars," Johnny said.

"Yeah, but we lost two men. One kilt and one wounded," Poke said.

"How do you know one was just wounded?" Gabe asked.

" 'Cause I seen him sittin' up as we was riding out," Poke replied.

"Yeah, I saw it too," Eddie said. Eddie was kneeling by the stream, filling his canteen. He stood up, corked it, then hooked it back onto his saddle pommel. "It was Carney, Johnny. He was the one that was wounded."

"Think he'll tell 'em where Last Chance is?" Pete asked.

"He won't tell them anything," Johnny said.

"How do you know?"

"Carney's not smart, but he's loyal," Johnny said. "He won't tell them anything."

"You know what I think?" Gabe said. "I think we ought to hit 'em again."

"What?" Eddie asked.

"I said let's hit them again."

"Why?" Pete asked. "We done took all the money they had."

"We took all they have now," Gabe said. "But we didn't take all they're goin' to have. You heard that banker fella say that they would have the money in the bank in time for the auction, didn't you?"

"Yeah, but it ain't there now," Pete said.

"We won't hit them now. We'll hit them when the money is there."

"Are you crazy?" Poke asked. "You want to go back and rob the same bank a second time? Nobody would be dumb enough to do that."

Johnny smiled. "That's right," he said. "Nobody would be dumb enough to do it, which is just why nobody will be expecting us to come back."

"Wait a minute," Eddie Jordan said. "Are you saying that we are going to go back?"

"That's exactly what I'm saying," Johnny said. "We are going back, first, to get my brother; then, we're going back again when the money is transferred."

"Whoa, hold on there. Nobody said nothin' about goin' back to get your brother," Poke said. "I can see maybe goin' back again to get the money. But not to get Carney."

Johnny lifted the money bag. "We agreed that I would get half the money, right?"

"Yeah," Poke said.

Johnny stuck his hand down inside. "I won't take half. I'll take one eighth of it, just like all of you. That means that instead of getting four hundred dollars, you'll all get over seven hundred dollars apiece. That's almost double."

"What about when we get the big money?" Gabe asked.

"Yeah, what about that?"

Johnny nodded. "All right," he agreed. "Whatever we take from the bank when the cattlemen's money comes in, we'll share equally." He pointed his finger. "But that is only if you help me get my brother back."

Gabe nodded. "I'll go along with that," he said.

"Wait," Pete said. "Gabe, are you sure you want to do this?"

"If you don't want to do it, don't do it," Gabe said. "It'll just be a bigger share for the rest of us."

"No," Pete said quickly. "I didn't say I wasn't goin' to do it."

Gene Nunlee got two men to help him carry the coffin outside and stand it up in front of the mortuary. The reason it took two men was because the body of the bank robber that Falcon shot was in it. Nunlee hung a sign around his neck.

DO YOU KNOW THIS MAN?

Several of the townspeople came by to view the corpse, most out of a sense of morbid curiosity, though some to see if they could identify him.

"His name is Snyder," Sylvester said. "I don't know what his first name is, but I've seen him in the Gold Strike a few times."

The sheriff picked up a tablet from his desk and looked at it, then nodded. "Yes," he said. "I've had two others who have made the same identification. One of them even supplied a first name. He said his name was Jerry Snyder."

"Could be," Sylvester agreed. "Like I say, I can't speak as to his first name, but I know his last name is Snyder."

"That's all I need to know," Gibson said. "We'll get the son of a bitch buried this afternoon."

"You're going to the funeral?" Frances asked.

Falcon shook his head. "He won't be having a funeral," he said. "Just a burying. And I plan to go to that, just as I did for Cardis."

"Would you explain why you would want to attend the burial of someone you have killed?"

Falcon thought about it for a moment.

Sighing, he stroked his jaw before he replied.

"I don't know if I can explain it," he said. "But it seems to me like the most important moment in any man's life is the moment that he dies. Snyder and I were on opposite sides of that moment, connected by a single thread, so to speak. It could have been me, instead of him, and one day, it may well be."

Frances was quiet for a moment, then she nodded. "I'm glad," she said.

"Glad?"

"Yes. I'm glad you are not going to the burial as some sort of bizarre victory ritual. If you don't mind, Gordon and I will go with you."

Nunlee didn't use the hearse for Snyder. He kept the hearse protected with a felt-lined tarpaulin cover, and each time he used it, he would have to clean it before covering it up again. He didn't mind doing that for the funerals he had for the respectable people of town. But he had no intention of doing it for an outlaw like Jerry Snyder.

Nailing the cover down on the unpainted wood coffin, Nunlee and his grave digger loaded the coffin onto the back of a wagon, then started through town to the cemetery. Several of the men, seeing the wagon pass, stopped and removed their hats, while the women bowed their heads, more from a sense of the fact that death comes to all than for respect for the body that lay in the plain coffin.

When Nunlee reached the cemetery, he saw Falcon MacCallister, and Frances and Gordon Martin, standing by the grave that his grave digger had already opened. He wasn't that surprised to see MacCallister, for MacCallister had also been there when he buried Cardis. But he was a little surprised to see the widow Frances Martin and her son, Gordon, there.

Falcon stood by with his hat off as the coffin was lowered into the grave.

"I forgot to ask you when we buried the other gentleman you killed," Nunlee said. "But would you like to say a few words over the grave?"

"No."

"Very well. Jesse, close the grave."

"Yes, sir, Mr. Nunlee," the grave digger said.

As Falcon, Frances, and Gordon were walking back to town, Sheriff Gibson came out to meet them. He was carrying a piece of paper, which he showed to Falcon.

"Someone found this note this morning," Gibson said, handing the paper to Falcon.

To the People of Laramie
I killed this man to get your attention. If you do not release my brother by sundown today, I will kill another of your citizens. And I will kill one citizen every day until my brother is free.

Johnny Purvis

"What does he mean he killed a man to get our attention?" Frances asked.

"It was Tooey Keith, Mrs. Martin. The note was found lying on his chest. His throat had been cut."

"Oh," Frances said. "Oh, no. Who would do such a thing? Tooey never hurt a soul."

"Tooey Keith?" Falcon asked.

"He is . . . or rather, he was a harmless old soul," Sheriff Gibson said. "He was the town drunk. He slept in the livery stable most of the time, and he supported himself by doing odd jobs around town. Some of the more generous folks used to feed him." He nodded toward Frances. "I know Mrs. Martin did."

"I can't imagine anyone being so cruel as to want to hurt a poor old man like Tooey."

"Johnny Purvis is that cruel," Gibson said. "And the bad thing is, if we are to believe his note, it won't stop with Tooey. He intends to kill again."

253

"What are you going to do about it, Sheriff?" Falcon asked.

"Well, for one thing, I intend to hire a couple of deputies to patrol the town at night," Gibson said. "And for another, I'm going to ask you, Mitchum, and Miss Coyle to move in together."

"Move in together?" Frances asked with a raised eyebrow.

"Well, sort of together," Gibson said. "You see, they are the only eyewitnesses to the bank robbery. We'll need their testimony in court in order to convict Carney. And I figure that Johnny knows this, which means he'll be trying to stop them."

"Where do you plan for us to stay, Sheriff?" Falcon asked. "With all the cattlemen in town, the hotel is filled."

"I know," Gibson said. "I haven't figured that out yet. I could put you all up at the jail, but I wouldn't want to have to do that."

"They can all stay with me," Frances said.

"Why, Mrs. Martin, you don't have that kind of room, do you?"

"I can make that much room," Frances said. "I'll move in with my son. Miss Coyle can have my room. And I can put a cot up in the parlor for Mr. Mitchum. Mr. MacCallister is already staying with me."

"That's very good of you," Gibson said.

"I will see to it that the county pays you."

"I'm not worried about getting paid," Frances said. "I just want to see justice done."

"How soon can they move in?" Gibson asked.

"I can have everything ready within half an hour," Frances promised.

EIGHTEEN

"I hate putting you out like this," Kathleen said at the dinner table that evening.

"I don't mind," Frances said. "I just hope that you find your room comfortable."

"Yes, it's quite comfortable, thank you."

Gordon reached for the potatoes.

"Gordon, ask, don't reach," Frances corrected.

"Can I have some more 'taters?"

"You mean 'may' you have some more 'potatoes,' and yes, you may," Frances said, passing the bowl of mashed potatoes to her son.

"Falcon, I can see now why you were so anxious to stay here instead of taking a room at the Gold Strike," Kathleen said. "It's so . . ." She looked at Frances. "Homey, here."

"Yes, my stay here has been very pleasant," Falcon said.

"Mr. MacCallister, how long do you think

we'll have to be here like this?" Mitchum asked.

"Just until after the trial, I would think," Falcon said.

"I don't understand what the need was. I have a perfectly good room behind the bank. All of my things are there: my books, my arrowhead collection, my pictures."

"I know it's inconvenient," Falcon said. "But the sheriff thinks that it will be safer for us if we are all together."

"I suppose he's right, but I, for one, will be glad when this trial is over and we can get back to our normal lives," Mitchum said.

"Are you running the bank now, Mr. Mitchum?" Frances asked.

"Yes, ma'am, I am. Mrs. Frazier hired me," he said proudly. "I am interviewing people now to come work as a teller. But I'm sure you can understand that not just anyone can be a bank teller. It requires a person of mathematical skill and an even disposition." He looked at Gordon. "Young man, it is an occupation that you might pursue in your future."

"No, sir," Gordon replied. "I'm sure it's a good job and all, but I want to be a railroad engineer, just like my pa was."

"Well, yes, of course, that is a very admirable position as well," Mitchum said.

"Poor Mrs. Frazier, losing her husband like that. I must call on her," Frances said.

"Yes, ma'am, given that you lost your own husband, I'm sure you would be a great comfort to her," Mitchum said.

"Would you care for some more coffee, Mr. Mitchum?" Frances asked.

"Yes, ma'am, if you don't mind," Mitchum said, holding out his cup.

"More coffee, Miss Coyle?"

"Yes, thank you."

"I understand you are an entertainer. A singer?" Frances asked as she poured the coffee.

"Yes. Well, I'm just singing in small places now, but one day I would like to perform in the theaters of New York."

"Why New York?"

"Because that is the center of the theatrical world," Kathleen explained.

"Oh. Then, I'm sure you will make it one day."

It was nearly midnight, and Falcon was asleep when he heard a light tap on his door. Getting out of bed, he moved to the door quickly, then opened it.

"Frances, do you really think . . ."

That was as far as he got. The woman in the nightgown, standing just outside his door, wasn't Frances. It was Kathleen Coyle.

"Oh, my. Were you expecting someone else?" Kathleen asked. A broad, almost mocking smile spread across her face.

"What are you doing here?" Falcon asked without answering her question.

Kathleen faked a pout. "What am I doing here? I don't recall you asking me that question when I came to your hotel room in Miles City."

"We aren't in a hotel now," he said.

"Well, aren't you going to invite me in?" Kathleen asked. "No more than I have on now, it's cold out here."

"No," Falcon said. "I'm not going to invite you in."

"You invited me in before."

"I know I did. But I shouldn't have," Falcon said. "And it's not something I intend to ever do again."

"Oh? What if I forced myself in, Falcon? Would you really make a scene?"

"Yeah, I would," Falcon said. He closed the door.

Kathleen stood just outside the door for a moment, as if shocked that he had closed her out. Then, with a shrug, she turned and started back to her room.

■ ■ ■ ■

Hearing voices, Frances got out of bed and walked over to the door. Opening it, she peeked out just as the door was closing behind Kathleen. She saw the beautiful young woman, wearing only a nightgown, walking down the hallway to her room.

"What is it, Mom?" Gordon asked sleepily from the bed behind her.

"Nothing," Frances said, wiping a tear as she came back to bed.

"You are awfully quiet this morning, Mrs. Martin," Falcon said at breakfast.

"Am I?" Frances replied. "I guess I just don't have anything to talk about." Her voice was almost clipped.

"I can't stay here all day," Mitchum said. "I have a bank to run."

"I have to go to work as well," Kathleen said. "Sylvester isn't going to pay me to hang around here all day."

"The sheriff said he would call for us this morning," Falcon said. "I think he wants to have someone with us all the time, or at least until after the trial."

Mitchum took a watch from his pocket and examined it. "I hope he gets here soon.

I like to be in the bank at least one hour before it opens."

"I'm sure he will be," Falcon said.

With breakfast finished, Frances began picking up the plates and silverware. Falcon helped her.

"No need for you to do this. I can take care of it. I don't need any help," Frances said.

"Have you stopped to think that I might want to help?" Falcon asked as he continued gathering the settings from the table. He followed her into the kitchen and put the dishes down on the counter. "What is it, Frances? What is going on?" he asked.

"Why should something be going on?" Frances replied.

"Come on," Falcon said. "Your voice is so sharp this morning it could cut paper. Are you nervous about us being here? Because if you are, I can certainly understand, and I'll talk to the sheriff about it."

"No need for that," Frances said. "I'm not nervous about you being here."

"Well, something is bothering you."

"Look, why don't you just go into the parlor and keep Miss Coyle company?" she said. "I'm sure that, after last night, she must be wondering why you are paying so much attention to me."

"After last night? What are you talking about?"

"I saw her," Frances said.

"You saw her? What did she say? What did she tell you?"

"She didn't tell me anything," Frances said. "She didn't need to. I saw her leaving your room."

"Oh. So that's it."

"Yes, that's it. I know I have no right to interfere with what you do. I mean, I told you that there could be nothing between us. But I do wish you would have more respect for me than to do something like that in my own house, and while my son is here."

"You saw her leaving," Falcon said. "Did you see her go into my room?"

"What?"

"Did you see her go into my room?"

"No, but I saw her leaving your room and . . ."

"No, you didn't."

"Mr. MacCallister, don't tell me what I saw," Frances said. "I know exactly what I saw."

"You saw her leaving, but you did not see her leaving my room," Falcon said.

"But I . . ." Frances started. She was interrupted by Falcon raising his finger.

"You didn't see her come out of my room,

because she was never in it," Falcon said. "She came to the room and knocked on the door, but I would not let her in."

"You didn't let her in?"

"No."

"I . . ." Frances said. She let the word die on her lips.

"Frances, you said yourself that there is nothing between us," Falcon said. "So I've no reason to lie to you. If you want, I'll call Kathleen in here and have her tell you herself."

Frances shook her head, then chuckled in embarrassment.

"I can't believe that I let a little thing like that upset me so," she said. "Falcon, I'm sorry. I certainly have no right to question you about anything you do."

Falcon chuckled as well. "Falcon, is it, and not Mr. MacCallister? Well, I'm glad you are calling me by my first name again," he said. "Mr. MacCallister had such a cold ring to it."

"Mr. MacCallister?" Mitchum called from the front room. "The sheriff is here."

"All right, I'll be right there," Falcon said.

NINETEEN

Sheriff Gibson and one of his new deputies were standing on the front porch when Falcon, Mitchum, and Kathleen stepped outside.

"Folks, I want you to meet Deputy Edwards," Gibson said. "He's going to be in the bank all day."

"We don't have any money in the bank," Mitchum said. "Nobody is going to rob a bank that has no money."

"I'm more interested in keeping you safe for now," Gibson said. "You are a witness to a murder, remember?"

"How can I forget?"

"And Falcon, if you don't mind, I'd like you to hang around the saloon and keep an eye on Miss Coyle, at least until after the trial." He smiled broadly. "Now, that's not asking too much, is it?"

"No," Falcon said. "That's not asking too much."

With Gibson on one side and Deputy Edwards on the other side, the little party started back toward town from Frances's boardinghouse. They had gone about two blocks when someone came running up the road, shouting.

"Sheriff Gibson! Sheriff Gibson! Sheriff Gibson!"

"Yes, Wales," Gibson called back. "What is it?"

"You'd better come down here, Sheriff," Wales said. "There's somethin' you need to see."

"Mitchum, you and Miss Coyle stay here with the deputy. Falcon, if you don't mind, you come with me."

"All right," Falcon said, following the sheriff and Wales.

Wales led them up the narrow path between Wales's Dry Goods and Clothing Store and Emma's Dress Making Shop. They stopped when they reached the back of the buildings.

"He's over there," Wales said, pointing.

"Who's over there?"

"It's Troy Garrison, Sheriff," Wales said.

"Troy Garrison?" the sheriff replied. "He works at the rolling mill, doesn't he?"

"Yes, sir. He's a shift foreman there. A good man too," Wales said. "Mrs. Wales and I have had him over to our place more than once for supper."

"I know he's a good man," Gibson said.

Garrison was wearing coveralls and a red flannel shirt. He was lying facedown in the alley almost hidden by a clump of weeds. The way his feet were turned out at an odd angle, and the stillness with which he was lying, clearly indicated that he was dead.

"When did you find him?" Gibson asked.

"Just a couple of minutes ago," Wales said. "I had just swept up the store and come out back here to throw out the sweepin's. That's when I saw him' lyin' over there."

"Did you touch him?"

"No. I yelled at him a couple of times, just to see if he had passed out back here or somethin'. And when I didn't get no answer, I came to get you."

Sheriff Gibson rolled Garrison over onto his back. Like Keith, his throat had been cut. And like Keith, there was a note pinned to his chest.

This is number two. If my brother isn't released by noon today, there will be more.
                                    Johnny Purvis

Gibson sighed. "I don't mind telling you that this is one son of a bitch I would love to see hang. Beggin' your pardon, Miss Coyle, for the language."

"Sheriff, I work in a saloon. I've heard such language before," Kathleen said.

"I should have killed him when I had the chance," Falcon said in dry, angry tones.

"You mean when he robbed the bank?" Sheriff Gibson asked.

"No. I mean when he broke into Miss Coyle's room up in Miles City. What I don't understand is why the sheriff didn't keep him up there. You'd think breaking and entering would be at least six months," Falcon said.

"Oh, well, uh, that's my fault, I suppose," Kathleen said.

"How is it your fault?"

"I didn't stop by the sheriff's office to press charges. I know I should have, but the whole experience was so unpleasant that I just didn't want to see him again. I guess, in a way, this is all my fault."

"Don't blame yourself. You had no way of knowing how everything was going to turn out," Gibson said. "And I can understand your not pressing charges. I've had trouble myself getting people to press charges, either from fear, or just because they didn't want to bother with a trial," Gibson said.

"Still, I feel responsible," Kathleen said.

"Come on," Gibson said to Falcon. "Let's get Mr. Mitchum and Miss Coyle where they are supposed to be; then I'll get Nunlee down here to take care of the body." He sighed. "Nunlee is doing quite a business lately."

"Did you check the horses?" Johnny asked as Pete came back into the camp.

"Yeah, I checked them. They're fine," Pete said. He sat down on a rock, pulled up a long piece of grass, and began sucking on the root. "Tell me, Johnny, just how much longer do you plan to keep this up?"

"How much longer do I plan to keep what up?" Johnny replied.

"You know what I'm talkin' about," Pete said. "This business of goin' into town ever' night and killin' someone. We ain't goin' to get away with this forever, you know."

"We've done fine so far," Johnny said.

"That's 'cause we ain't been seen. But you been leavin' them letters, tellin' the whole world we're the ones doin' it. That means we're goin' to hang for sure if we ever get caught."

Johnny laughed, a short, bitter laugh. "What the hell, Pete? Do you think we won't hang now if we get caught? We kilt that banker, remember?"

"Another thing," Pete said. "I prob'ly got me more money in my saddlebag now than I've ever had at one time in my whole life. What's the good of havin' all that money if I can't spend none of it?"

"What would you spend it on if you was in town?" Gabe asked.

"I don't know. Whiskey maybe. And a whore. Yeah, I'd get me a whore, that's for sure." He looked at the spitted rabbit that was cooking over the fire. "And a good dinner."

"Think about it, Pete. If you just don't lose your patience, if you stick around and see this thing through to the end, you won't be spendin' it on no one whore. Hell, you can buy yourself an entire whorehouse."

Pete smiled. "Yeah, I hadn't thought about it like that, but that's right, ain't it? I could buy myself a whorehouse and just have anyone I wanted, anytime I wanted."

"And buy your own restaurant too, if you wanted one."

"Yeah, well, now buyin' a restaurant might not be a bad idea. 'Cause I'm sure as hell gettin' tired of eatin' squirrel an' rabbit and the like."

Gabe leaned over the fire and stuck the

point of his knife into the roasting rabbit. "This here looks about done," he said.

"Rabbit is a hell of a breakfast for a rich man to be eatin' now, ain't it?" Pete said. "I want a steak."

"Hey, Pete, if you don't want your share of the rabbit, I'll eat it," Eddie said.

"I didn't say I wasn't goin' to eat it," Pete growled. "I just said I was tired of it. And I was just wonderin' why we're doin' all this for Johnny's brother, when we should be plannin' to hit the bank again."

"That's exactly what we are doin'," Johnny answered. "There ain't none of this about my brother." Johnny carved off a piece of rabbit.

"What do you mean there ain't none of this about your brother?" Pete asked. "It's all about your brother."

"No, it ain't," Johnny said. He blew on the meat a few times, cooling it, before he took a bite.

"Then what is it about?"

"It's about the same thing it's always been about," Johnny said. "It's about robbin' the bank. You see, the thing is, we keep hittin' 'em about my brother, pretty soon they're goin' to forget all about the bank. So even though we've robbed it before, we'll be able to walk in there a second time just as pretty as you please. There won't nobody in town be expectin' us to come back."

The topics of conversation in the Gold Strike were Tooey Keith and Troy Garrison.

"I don't know if any of you gentlemen remember the time that cowboy from the Double X dropped a quarter into the spittoon and told Tooey he could have it if he would stick his hand down in the spittoon to get it out," Nye said.

"Yeah," Sylvester said. He chuckled. "At first, I was pissed off at the cowboy for doin' something like that. I started to say something too, but Tooey just held up his hand, as if tellin' me to wait. Then, he emptied the spittoon and cleaned it out before he got the quarter back."

"Yes," Nye said, laughing. "The cowboy got real mad, and tried to take his quarter back. He said Tooey didn't do what he was supposed to do."

"That's when you told the cowboy you was a lawyer and that in your opinion Tooey had fulfilled his end of the contract," Clyde said.

"The cowboy just looked real strange and said, 'What contract?' " Sylvester said, laughing. "Then you told him — what was it exactly that you told him?"

271

"I simply told him," Nye said, picking up the story from there, "that his offer constituted a verbal contract, enforceable in any court in the land. And that his contract stated only that Tooey was to stick his hand down into the spittoon. It said nothing about sticking his hand into the mess."

"That cowboy looked like he had been shot," Clyde said. "You know, I do believe it was his last quarter."

"I'm sure it was," Sylvester said. "I know he didn't spend another dime in here that night."

Sylvester, Clyde, and Nye laughed as they recalled the cowboy's reaction to the joke that had backfired.

"Troy Garrison was a good man too," Clyde said.

"I didn't know Mr. Garrison that well," Sylvester said.

"I knew him really well. We worked together," Clyde said.

"Yes, I knew he worked down at the rolling mill, but I don't know that I ever saw him come in here."

Clyde shook his head. "No, and you wouldn't," he said. "Garrison was a teetotaler."

Sylvester nodded. "That would explain it, I reckon."

"He was from Missouri, and his father was a drunk. His father used to beat him up when he was a kid. He used to beat up his mother too. Then one day, after his father half-killed his mother, Troy picked up a shotgun and blew his father away," Nye said.

"Damn! I never knew that," Clyde said. "I mean I saw him every day, and I never knew that."

"No," Nye said. "Nobody in town knew it. Mr. Garrison came to me a couple of years ago, and said he wanted to get it off his chest. He asked me if I thought he should go back to Missouri and confess."

"What did you tell him?" Sylvester asked.

"I told him to just leave it be, and that if anything ever came of it, I would defend him pro bono."

"Pro bono? What does that mean?" Clyde asked.

"It means I would defend him for free."

"How old was Garrison when he did that?" Sylvester asked.

"I think he told me he was fifteen."

"That's a hell of a burden for a fifteen-year-old to have to carry around with him."

"Yes, it is. He left home immediately after it happened, then started wandering around until he wound up here. He never went home again," Nye said.

"Hell of a way for him to wind up," Sylvester said. "Facedown in the alley like that."

"At least he wasn't married," Nye said. "It would have been even more tragic if he left a widow behind."

"That's true," Sylvester said. "Neither one of them were married."

Sylvester looked down toward the end of the bar where Kathleen was sitting. She had a very pale expression on her face. "Kathleen, are you all right?"

"I'm fine," Kathleen said in a weak voice. "I just feel a little dizzy, is all."

"It's our fault for talking about such things," Sylvester said. "We won't talk about 'em no more."

At noon, Sheriff Gibson stuck his head in through the saloon door.

"Falcon, Miss Coyle, I'll take you two to lunch now," he said.

"We could eat here," Kathleen suggested.

"Now, why would you want to eat saloon food, when you could eat Mrs. Martin's food?" Gibson asked.

Falcon chuckled. "Sheriff, sounds to me like Mrs. Martin has offered to feed you as well."

"Me and my deputy," Gibson said enthusiastically.

"Where's Mitchum?" Falcon asked as he, Gibson, and Kathleen left the saloon.

"Mr. Mitchum is still at the bank. Edwards is with him. We'll stop by and pick them up on the way down to Mrs. Martin's boarding-house."

Mitchum was smiling broadly when Falcon and the others went in.

"I have great news," Mitchum said. "The money that was stolen has been replaced."

"Replaced? How?" Kathleen asked.

"Our bank belongs to a mutual co-operative with several other banks. We have an insurance policy in effect that can replace money lost in a robbery," Mitchum said. "I'm proud to say that not one depositor lost money as a result of the robbery."

"Well, the citizens of the town will be happy to hear that," Gibson said. "Oh, and I see you have someone new working with you."

"Yes. This is Abner Brookfield," Mitchum said. "He arrived from Denver this morning. He is well experienced in the banking profession and will assume the job of teller."

"Good. Then you've got someone you can leave in charge while we all go to lunch," Sheriff Gibson said.

"Yes, he can handle the position quite

well," Mitchum said. "Mr. Brookfield, I will be back within the hour."

"Yes, sir, Mr. Mitchum."

Leaving the bank, the five started toward the Martin house. They were met halfway there by young Gordon, who came running up to meet them.

"There he is," Falcon said, greeting the young man with a smile. "Gordon Martin, the fastest runner in Albany County."

"Hello, Mr. MacCallister, Sheriff, Miss Coyle," Gordon said. "Mom sent me to the store to buy a can of peaches." He smiled broadly. "Guess what? We're having fried peach pies for supper. Do you like fried peach pies?"

"Who doesn't like fried peach pies?" Falcon said.

"They are my favorite thing," Gordon said.

Suddenly, they heard the sound of thundering hooves and, turning toward the sound, saw eight mounted horsemen galloping down the middle of the street.

"What in the world is going on?" Gibson asked. "Is that a bunch of drunken cowboys?"

"I'll tell them to slow down, Sheriff," Edwards said, starting toward the middle of the street to signal them.

"Deputy, no!" Falcon shouted, recognizing one of the riders then. "It's Johnny Purvis!"

Concurrent with Falcon's warning, the horsemen drew their guns and began firing. Deputy Edwards went down.

Falcon and the sheriff both started shooting back. Falcon got one and the sheriff got another, but at that moment a freight wagon was rumbling into town and Johnny managed to maneuver his men behind it. Using the wagon for cover, the six remaining riders were able to dart up between two buildings, getting them out of the line of fire. They crossed the railroad track, then put the depot between them and the town as they rode away across the prairie.

Putting his gun away, Falcon turned back toward the others. That was when he saw that both Mitchum and Gordon were down.

"Gordon!" Falcon shouted, running to the side of the boy.

"Did you get any of them?" Gordon asked, his voice weak with pain and shock.

"Yes," Falcon said. "So did the sheriff."

"Good," Gordon said. "Tell Mom I guess there'll be no fried peach pie for me," he said in a strained voice. He took one last, gasping breath, then stopped breathing.

TWENTY

From *The Sentinel:*

MORE VIOLENCE PLAGUES OUR CITY.
Mounted Gunmen Ride Through City!
Four of the Assailants are Killed.
EDWARDS AND MITCHUM GUNNED
DOWN.
Young Gordon Martin among the Dead.
By JAMES HAYFORD, Publisher.

The battlefields of the U. S. Cavalry, engaged in mortal combat with the Indians, hold no sway over the streets of Laramie. Indeed, of late, we could compete with some of the great battles of the War of Rebellion so recently fought. Laramie now has the dubious distinction of having come to the notice of the great metropolises of the East, where such cities as Chicago, St. Louis, Philadelphia, and New York fill their pages with stories of the violence taking place in our streets.

One might think there is pride in such recognition, but that is not the case, for our notoriety comes from our bloody history of recent days.

On Wednesday of this week, eight riders, among them, one Johnny Purvis, bank robber and brother of a prisoner about to face trial, rode into town. They sprayed the town with deadly gunfire, killing Deputy Edwards and Banker Mitchum. They also killed young Gordon Martin, son of the Widow Martin, who runs a boardinghouse on the west end of town.

Our readers may remember young Gordon as the lad who won the footrace in the series of athletic events so recently held. That so young and vibrant a life could be so cruelly cut down accrues to the shame of us all.

Readers may also remember from the last edition of The SENTINEL that two of our citizens, Troy Garrison and Tooey Keith, were found murdered, with notes affixed, demanding the release of the bank robber now in custody. It is believed that those who so brazenly assaulted our town are the selfsame people who came in the night to murder the two aforementioned souls.

Funerals for the three who fell before the villains' guns will be held on Thursday of this week. Because of the public sympathy for the bereaved, it is believed that the aggregate of these funerals may be the largest in Laramie's history, if not indeed in the entire history of Wyoming.

Because there was only one hearse, the funerals of Edwards, Mitchum, and Gordon were carried out at three different times. Gordon's funeral was the last, and perhaps because he was the youngest, it was the largest. The population of Laramie was two thousand people, and nearly all lined the street to watch the hearse drive by, Gordon's glossy-black coffin clearly visible through the glass sides of the hearse.

Frances, dressed in black, with a long, black veil, rode in an open carriage behind the hearse. Her brother-in-law, Cody, was riding with her, his arm around her shoulders. As the hearse passed by, the spectators moved out into the street to follow the ever-growing cortege to the cemetery. There, they stood by as the Reverend E. D. Owen conducted the funeral.

"A reading from the Sixty-first Psalm," Owen said. "I will abide in thy tabernacle forever. I will trust in the covert of thy wings. For thou, oh, God, has heard my vows: thou has given me the heritage of those that fear thy name. Thou wilt prolong the kin's life: and his years as many generations. He shall abide before God forever: Oh, prepare mercy and truth, which may preserve him."

When the preacher finished with his reading, Frances stepped forward and sprinkled a handful of dirt on top of the coffin. Then the coffin was lowered into the ground.

"Ashes to ashes, dust to dust, we commit the body of thy servant Gordon O'Neil Martin, in the sure and certain hope of his resurrection and life eternal in the blessed arms of Our Lord. Amen."

Sheriff Gibson stepped over to Frances as the funeral concluded.

"Mrs. Martin, I can't begin to express my condolences to you. Gordon was a fine, fine boy." He shook his head. "No, he wasn't a boy, he was a fine young man."

"Thank you, Sheriff Gibson," Frances replied in a choked voice.

"If there is anything I can do . . ."

"I'm fine, thank you," Frances said.

Nodding, Gibson left the cemetery and

hurried down to the depot, reaching there even as he heard the afternoon train arriving. The train pulled into the station with steam venting and brakes squealing as the huge, lumbering engine ground to a halt. It sat there for several seconds before the first passenger disembarked, an older gray-haired woman. She looked around in some confusion and, because she was dressed like an Easterner, Gibson knew at once that everything here was probably very strange to her.

"Mama, oh, Mama, you did come!" a woman called out in excitement, hurrying to meet the older woman.

"Dora, what in heaven's name possesses you to live in a place like this?" the older woman complained. "I've had a miserable trip."

"Oh, but Mama, wait until you see the ranch," Dora said. "You'll love it."

Dora was, Gibson knew, the wife of Dan Pratt, a very successful rancher who lived about five miles out of town.

As the rest of the passengers disembarked, Sheriff Gibson saw the man he had come to meet, Judge Jacob Blair.

"Judge Blair, over here," Gibson called.

Judge Blair was a tall, thin man, clean-shaven and with silver hair. Answering

Gibson's summons, he came over to shake the sheriff's hand.

"Did you have a good trip?" Gibson asked.

"I came forty miles in but two hours," Blair said. "How could it not be good?"

"Forty miles in two hours," Gibson replied. "We do live in marvelous times."

"Indeed we do. So, Sheriff Gibson, do you have a place for me to stay? I have been led to believe that every room in the hotel is booked up."

"That's true, Your Honor, the hotel is booked," Gibson said. "But I have made arrangements for you, if you don't mind sleeping in a room above the saloon."

The judge laughed. "Well, that depends. Will I be sharing the room with one of the soiled doves?"

Gibson laughed as well. "I'm afraid not, Your Honor."

"Damn," Judge Blair teased. "I was rather looking forward to that."

"I'll get your grip," Gibson offered, picking up the carpetbag.

As Sheriff Gibson and Judge Blair walked down the sidewalk toward the Gold Strike, the judge noticed that many of the buildings were draped with black bunting.

"What is all the bunting for?" he asked.

"Well, Judge, maybe you haven't heard,

but there have been eleven people killed here in the last three weeks."

"Eleven?" Billing pursed his lips and gave out a low whistle. "My, oh, my. I knew you had experienced some difficulty here. I had no idea that eleven had been killed. What about the fellow I am to try? Is he charged with the murders?"

"Just one of the murders, Your Honor. Though his brother has been trying to force us to release him, and he is responsible for at least five more."

"Well, you can hang a man for one killing, or for five," Blair said. "Either way, he's dead."

"How soon do you intend to start the trial?" Gibson asked.

"I take it that the defendant is not represented by counsel?"

"No, Your Honor."

"I will need to meet with all of the lawyers in town so that I can choose both the defense and prosecuting attorney. And they will need a few days to get prepared for the case. We'll have the trial as soon as we can get it all arranged."

"It can't be too soon to suit me," Gibson said.

The number of killings in and around

Laramie had, as Hayford reported in his newspaper, drawn national attention, and reporters from a dozen newspapers had come to Laramie to cover the trial. Because of the shortage of hotel rooms, they had to be put up in various places around town, with James Hayford making most of the arrangements for them. Four of the reporters were staying with Frances Martin, two of them sharing her room, and two sleeping on cots in the parlor. Frances moved again into Gordon's room.

"Are you sure you want to do this?" Falcon asked, stepping into the kitchen as Frances was preparing supper.

"Do what?" Frances asked.

"Have this many people stay in your house. I would think you might want some time alone. In fact, I was willing to move out myself, if you wanted me to." He held up his hand. "Oh, of course, I would pay the full amount we agreed upon."

"No, don't do that," Frances said. "I'm glad you are here. The others too. If I couldn't stay busy, all I would do is sit around all day and cry."

"I understand," Falcon said. "My wife has been dead for many years now, but sometimes it's almost as if I can hear her laughter in the wind. And at night, there are times when I can still feel her warm body next to mine."

"How did you get through it, Falcon?" Frances asked. "How do you get rid of the pain in your soul? Where did you go for help?"

Falcon put his hand gently on Frances's shoulder. "You will learn, Frances, that you can't go anywhere for help. It is a journey you must take alone. But in these few days I have been here, I have come to know you, and I know you have the strength to get through this," Falcon said.

"I don't want to be strong," Frances said. She leaned against Falcon and put her head on his chest. He could feel her quiet sobs, though she was doing a good job of suppressing them.

After a moment or two, she pulled away from him and wiped her nose with the handkerchief she held clutched in her hand.

"I know you say that no one can help," she said. "But I do thank you for being here."

"Excuse me, madam," one of the reporters said, sticking his head into the kitchen at that moment. "But I was wondering if . . . that is, we were wondering . . . if you had any coffee prepared. We could drink it as we await our dinner."

"Go back and sit down," Falcon said. "I'll bring you some coffee."

"Thank you, that is very nice of you," the reporter said.

Falcon helped Frances serve dinner, then held the chair for her before sitting down himself. The reporters had been discussing the local story, as well as several other events.

"MacCallister," the reporter from New York said. "I seem to know that name."

"I'm sure it's a fairly common name," Falcon said.

"Wait, I know what it is," the reporter said. "There is an acting team in the New York theater, quite well known they are. Andrew and Rosanna MacCallister. I believe, in fact I am sure, that they are husband and wife."

Falcon shook his head. "They are brother and sister," he said.

The New York reporter laughed. "Really, Mr. MacCallister. And just how would someone like you know that?"

"Because they are my brother and sister," Falcon said.

"You don't say." It was obvious by the tone of the reporter's voice that he didn't believe Falcon.

Falcon chuckled. "Surely you don't think

I would brag about having relatives in New York, do you?" Falcon asked, and the other reporters, all of whom were from Western areas, laughed.

"Mr. Caulder, I can't believe you don't know who Mr. MacCallister is," Stanley Morgan said. Morgan was from the Denver newspaper.

"Good heavens," Caulder said. "You aren't going to tell me that this big galoot is an actor as well."

"Hardly," Morgan said. "But he is one of the best-known pistoleros in the West. Some say he is better than Wild Bill Hickock ever was, that he is superior to Wyatt Earp, or Clay Allison, or Temple Houston."

"Oh, my," Caulder said. "Are you what they call a gunfighter? Have you ever killed anyone, Mr. MacCallister?"

"For God's sake, Caulder, didn't you do any research at all before you left New York?" Morgan asked.

"Yes," MacCallister said. "I've killed."

"How many?"

"I don't think that is anything you need to know."

"It's a morbid question, I admit, and I apologize for asking," Caulder said. "It is just that, before I came out here, I did a story about the Phantom Sharpshooter of

Devil's Den. So I have such things on my mind. I'm sure that's why my editor sent me here to cover the many shootings that have taken place."

"Who is the Phantom Sharpshooter of Devil's Den?" one of the other reporters asked.

"Well, that's just it. Nobody really knows, actually." Caulder replied. "Oh, we know his name, and we know he is a New Yorker, but that's all we know about him. He seems to have just disappeared after the war, and all efforts to find him have proven fruitless."

"What is his name?"

"His name is Fitzpatrick O'Neil. He is an Irishman."

"An Irishman, was he?" Morgan asked. He laughed. "And tell me now, Mr. Caulder, what are the odds of someone named Fitzpatrick O'Neil being Irish?"

The others laughed as well.

"What did you find out about O'Neil?"

"Practically nothing," Caulder replied. "Except for the remarkable job of shooting he did during the Battle of Gettysburg. It is said that he killed twenty-three rebels in a single afternoon, every victim taken with a single shot from a distance of over three hundred yards."

"Twenty-three in a single afternoon?"

Morgan replied with a whistle. "I think that would make even our most productive gunman take notice. What do you think, Mr. MacCallister?"

"I think Mr. O'Neil probably has some ghosts to deal with," Falcon said in a tone of voice that indicated he knew what he was talking about.

"Gentlemen, I hate to interrupt this spirited conversation," Frances said. "But I'm going to have to clear the table so I can get the dishes washed for breakfast in the morning."

"A most reasonable request, madam," Caulder said. "I must write my first report anyway. I'll work on it tonight. Good night, gentlemen."

"Good night," the others said.

The others left, but Falcon remained at the table.

"May I help you?" he asked.

"No need," Frances said. "I can do it myself."

"I didn't ask if you needed me to help," Falcon said. "I was asking your permission to let me help."

Frances chuckled. "Well, of course you can help if you want to."

"I want to," Falcon said, picking up several of the plates and carrying them in to the kitchen.

"I'll wash, you dry," Frances said. She had been heating water on the stove and she poured this into one dishpan, to which she added soap. Another pan beside it held clear water for rinsing.

"Can you believe there are so many reporters here?" Frances said as she began washing the dishes.

"We seem to have drawn them," Falcon replied as he took the first plate to dry. "Where do I put this?"

"Just stack them on the sideboard. I'll be using them for breakfast."

"The reporter from New York is quite a talkative fellow."

"He's rather typical of New Yorkers, though," Frances said.

"Have you met many New Yorkers?"

"I was born and raised in New York City," Frances said.

"You were? I didn't know that."

Frances chuckled. "Given your apparent disdain for New York, I thought it best not to tell you."

"I have no disdain for New York. You heard me tell the reporter that my brother and sister are there. Besides, I fought against some New York Regiments during the war. I know what good men they were."

"You fought for the South?"

"Yes."

"I was for the North."

"I figured as much. I had a brother who fought for the North."

"Such is the tragedy," Frances said. "I guess there were a lot of families divided by the war."

"What brought you to the West?" Falcon asked.

"I got married after the war. My husband was a railroad man, and he was excited by the prospect of being able to cross this entire country by train. He signed on with the Union Pacific, and we wound up out here."

"You said he was killed in a railroad accident?"

"Yes. A trestle across Dead Horse Gulch gave way, and his engine fell about two hundred feet."

"I'm sorry."

A tear slid down her cheek. "At least he is with Gordon now," she said.

TWENTY-ONE

From the pen of Lee Caulder:

Special to the New York Standard.

LARAMIE, WYOMING TERRITORY. The first thing one notices when stepping down from the train in Laramie is that the entire city is blanketed in a pall of smoke. The smoke emanates from the rolling mill, a huge, exceedingly ugly edifice which houses the machinery for making steel rails. The people of Laramie are quite proud of this factory as it employs well over a hundred of their fellow citizens.

The next thing one notices is the horrible odor that permeates the entire town. For the most part, this is due to the condition of the streets, filled as they are with droppings from the horses, mules, and draft oxen that ply their ways in pursuit of commerce. It is also due to the fact that the city has no sanitary department to speak of, and thus refuse of all description is allowed to collect at various points around the town.

But for all this, Laramie is now the center of attention for much of the nation. It has achieved this level of prominence from the fact that, within the last three weeks, nine men have been shot down in the streets. Two more men have died by the piteous method of having had their throats cut.

And who is responsible for all the violence? If the prosecutor and the people of the town are to have their way, the responsibility will fall upon the head, or perhaps I should say the neck, of a man named Carney.

I am sorry, dear readers, that I cannot give you more of a name than that. From the moment of his capture, Carney has refused to disclose his entire name, though it is believed that his name might be Carney Purvis. This belief is fostered by the fact that the leader of the violent gang to which Carney belonged is Johnny Purvis. Purvis has instigated a series of murders, and in a bit of vainglory, has left notes penned to the bodies of his victims in which he demands the release of his brother, Carney.

Of course, one could make the case that he is using the term "brother" in the same way that various gangs of ruffians have referred to themselves as a "brotherhood," thus including all who belong as their brother. But most believe that in this case, Carney really is the biological brother of Johnny Purvis.

The trial of Carney Purvis begins at one o'clock on the fifth instant, and your intrepid reporter will be present from the fall of the judge's gavel until the end of the trial. Although seats in the courthouse are at a premium, some have been set aside for the many reporters present, and by my pen, you, my dear reader, shall be able to follow the entire event, word by word.

Immediately after breakfast the next morning, Caulder hurried to the railroad depot in order to make arrangements to send to his editor, by wire, the story he had written the night before.

"Do you plan to do this every day?" the telegrapher asked, looking at the message.

"I do," Caulder said.

The telegrapher whistled, and shook his

head. "That is going to cost you a lot of money," he said.

Caulder smiled. "No, my good man," he replied. "That is going to cost my editor a lot of money."

The Albany County Courthouse was a substantial, two-story brick building with long, narrow arched windows and doors. It was surrounded by poplar trees that were in full foliage, thus providing some shade for the building.

Even before the trial started, staff workers had gone about with long, hooked poles, drawing the windows down from the top, and lifting them from the bottom, thus providing cross ventilation, which, with the shade of the trees, made the courtroom very pleasant.

The door to the courtroom was opened at twelve-thirty, one half hour before the trial was to begin. Sheriff Gibson and two of his deputies stood at the door, taking the guns from all who entered.

"What do you mean I can't come in here wearin' my gun?" one of the cowboys asked. "I wear my gun ever'where I go."

"And you can still wear it everywhere you go," Sheriff Gibson said. "You just can't wear it in this courtroom."

The cowboy wasn't the only one to complain, but like the cowboy, everyone who was asked to shed their guns did so.

"Falcon, I hate to ask you to get shed of your gun," the sheriff said. "I asked Judge Blair if I could appoint you a temporary deputy, but because you are a witness, he said that it wouldn't be proper."

"I understand," Falcon said. He removed his pistol and handed it, handle first, to the sheriff.

"Do you have a holdout gun?" the sheriff asked.

Falcon hesitated for a moment, then pulled the double-barrel derringer from his boot and handed it over as well.

"I'm sorry," Gibson said again.

"You're just doing your duty, Sheriff," Falcon said as he went inside the courtroom to take a seat. Because he was a witness, a seat was reserved for him in the first row, where he sat next to Kathleen.

"Oyez, oyez, oyez, this court in and for the County of Albany is now in session, the Honorable Judge Jacob Blair, presiding. God bless the United States of America, the Territory of Wyoming, and this honorable court! All rise," the court bailiff shouted.

The gallery of the court was packed, with

every seat occupied. There was a scraping of feet and rustle of clothing as all stood.

Wearing a black robe, Judge Blair entered the courtroom from a door in front, stood behind the bench for a moment, then sat down.

"Be seated," he said.

The spectators sat.

"What is the purpose of this court?" the judge asked.

"Your Honor, there comes before this honorable court one Carney, who is charged with bank robbery, and for the murder of Gene Frazier," the bailiff announced.

"Carney? Is that a first name or a last name?"

"We don't know, Your Honor," the bailiff replied. "The only name he would give us is Carney."

"Mr. Carney, what is your name?" Judge Blair asked.

"Carney," Carney replied, and there was a smattering of laughter through the court.

Judge Blair slammed his gavel down. "Order in the court," he said sternly. "Very well, let the record reflect that the man we are trying" — he paused for a moment and stared directly at Carney — "and the man we may ultimately hang, shall be known only as Carney."

"You think my brother's a'goin' to let you hang me?" Carney asked. "I can tell you right now, he ain't a'goin' to allow it."

"Mr. Carney, one more outburst from you, and I will have you bound and gagged. Do you understand that?"

Carney didn't answer.

"Do you understand that, sir?" Judge Blair asked in a louder and more commanding voice.

"Yeah," Carney said.

"You do mean, 'Yes, Your Honor,' do you not?" Judge Blair asked.

Carney didn't answer.

"You do mean 'Yes, Your Honor,' do you not?" Blair repeated.

Carney still didn't answer.

"Sheriff, get manacles and a gag."

"Yes, Your Honor!" Carney said quickly.

Blair waited for a moment; then he looked at Sheriff Gibson. "You may stand down, Sheriff," he said. "Counsel for the defense, if you do not keep your client in check, I will hold you in contempt. Do you understand that?"

"Yes, Your Honor," the lawyer sitting beside Carney said.

"Very good. Now, will counsel for defense publish his name and qualifications?"

The lawyer sitting beside Carney stood. "I

am counsel for the defense, Your Honor, appointed by the court. My name is Anthony Norton, duly authorized by the bar of Wyoming to practice law."

"Very good," Judge Blair said. "Is prosecution present?"

Bill Nye stood. "I have been appointed by the county prosecutor to act as prosecutor, Your Honor. I am Bill Nye."

"Mr. Nye, I trust that you will not, in the middle of this trial, write a letter to the President of the United States tendering your resignation."

The gallery, knowing that the question was in reference to Nye's letter resigning as postmaster, laughed out loud and Judge Blair, because he had made the joke, not only allowed the laughter, but joined in.

"I will see the case through, Your Honor."

"Aren't we the lucky ones, though?" Judge Blair said sarcastically. "All right, Mr. Prosecutor, I invite you to make your case."

"Thank you, Your Honor," Nye said.

As Nye walked over to begin his presentation to the jury, Falcon noticed that the jury was composed of men and women. For a moment it startled him. Then he remembered having read that Wyoming was the only state or territory in the nation that allowed women to vote, as well as serve on a jury.

"Ladies," Nye said, beginning his presentation. He made a slight bow to them, and Falcon noticed that the four women on the jury nodded their heads back at him. "And gentlemen of the jury. There are, in this city today, women who have been deprived of their husbands, children deprived of their fathers, and even a grieving mother, deprived of her child. . . ."

"I object, Your Honor!" Norton shouted.

"You are objecting to my opening statement?" Nye said, turning away from the jury.

"Mr. Norton, to what are you objecting?" Judge Blair asked.

"I'm objecting to counsel's mention of the number of widows and fatherless children in Laramie," Norton said.

"Are you making the claim that the statement is false?" Nye asked. He pointed to the row of newspaper journalists who were busy taking notes. "Surely you don't think newspapermen came from all over the country just to cover the trial of your client? Your objection is denied."

"You are out of order, Mr. Nye," Judge Blair said sternly. "I will rule on the objection."

301

"I was just trying to help out, Your Honor," Nye said, and the gallery laughed.

"Objection denied," Blair said.

"Thank you, Your Honor," Nye replied. Turning to the jury, he continued his opening remarks, speaking for another five minutes before ending it with the statement that ". . . after all the facts are in evidence, I feel certain that you will find the defendant guilty of murder in the first degree."

Norton didn't approach the jury, but spoke from his position behind the defendant's table.

"Despite the prosecutor's brazen attempt to suggest that my client was, in some way, responsible for the fact that there are many widows and fatherless children in Laramie now, I hope you realize that he is being tried for one murder, and one murder alone. And I intend to present evidence that will introduce doubt as to whether Mr. Carney was personally responsible for the death of Mr. Frazier."

Norton held up his finger for a long moment, as if asking the jury to focus on his next statement. "And I remind you that the law requires you to be satisfied, *beyond the shadow of a doubt,* as to the guilt of a person, before you can find him guilty. If you cannot find him guilty, beyond the shadow of a doubt, you must acquit. Thank you."

Norton sat down, and Nye called his first witness.

"Prosecution calls Mr. Falcon MacCallister to the stand."

Falcon walked to the front of the court, raised his right hand, and was sworn in as a witness.

"Would you please tell the court in your own words what happened on Thursday, July 17th, of the year current?"

Falcon told how he had come into the bank with Miss Kathleen Coyle. He said also that the bank was empty except for the bank owner, Mr. Frazier, and the bank teller, Mr. Mitchum.

"They were standing at the front window, looking at the fire," Falcon added.

"And what fire would that be?" Nye asked.

"The feed store had been set on fire by the bank robbers in order to create a diversion," Falcon said.

"Objection, Your Honor, the witness has made a conclusion based on facts not in evidence. We don't know that the bank robbers started the fire."

"Sustained," Judge Blair said.

"Mr. MacCallister, how do you know that

the bank robbers started the fire?" Nye asked.

"Purvis told us he started the fire," Falcon answered.

"Objection, Your Honor, hearsay," Norton said.

"Sustained. The jury will disregard the comment referring to who started the fire. Abandon this particular line of questioning, Mr. Nye."

"Yes, Your Honor. Go ahead with your narrative, Mr. MacCallister."

"We, that is, Miss Coyle and I, were getting ready to conduct our business, when six masked men came into the bank."

"Was Carney one of the six?"

"He was."

"Objection, Your Honor. If the men were masked, how can he be sure Carney was one of them?"

"That's a good question, Your Honor," Nye said. "May I ask that of my witness?"

"By all means, Mr. Nye."

"If the men were masked, how do you know that one of them was Carney?" Nye asked Falcon.

"Well, for one thing, look at him," Falcon said. "You don't see many men as large as he is. And for another, he and Johnny Purvis pulled their masks down while they were in the bank."

"So you saw his face during the robbery?"

"I did."

"Withdraw the objection, Your Honor," Norton said.

"Good. That saves me the trouble of having to overrule it," Blair said.

Falcon continued with his narrative, describing the consternation of the robbers when they learned that the bank didn't have as much money as they thought it should have. He concluded his testimony with the shooting of Gene Frazier.

"Mr. MacCallister, did Carney shoot Gene Frazier?"

"Yes."

"Thank you. Your witness, Counselor."

Norton approached the witness.

"Mr. MacCallister, the bank robbery took place on what day?"

"The 17th of July," Falcon replied.

"Is that the first time you ever saw Mr. Carney?"

"No."

"No?"

"No."

"So you had seen him before?"

"Yes."

"Where did you see him?"

"In the Gold Strike Saloon."

"And what was the occasion of that meeting?"

"I beg your pardon?"

"The meeting that you and Mr. Carney had in the Gold Strike, prior to the bank robbery. Would you say that the meeting was convivial?"

Falcon chuckled, then shook his head. "No, I wouldn't say it was friendly."

"In fact, didn't you and Mr. Carney have an altercation? And didn't he give you a black eye?"

"Your Honor, I object!" Nye said. "Whether or not Mr. MacCallister saw Carney before the bank robbery is irrelevant."

"I can establish relevancy, Your Honor," Norton said quickly.

"Then by all means, Counselor, please do so," Judge Blair said.

"It calls into question this witness's objectivity," Norton said. "After all, if he had his eye blackened by my client in an episode of fisticuffs, he might be looking for some way of extracting revenge."

"You are an idiot, Mr. Norton," the judge said.

"I beg your pardon, Your Honor?" Norton replied in a huff.

"Do you have any idea who Falcon Mac-

Callister is?"

"I . . . I seem to have heard the name," Norton said.

"You seem to have heard the name," Judge Blair said scornfully. "Well, let me tell you, Mr. Norton, Falcon MacCallister has earned a reputation for honesty and fair play. Based upon what I know about the man, I can say that your worries as to whether or not he is testifying in some manner to seek revenge against Carney is without foundation. The objection is sustained. Go to another line of questioning."

"Yes, Your Honor," Norton said. Then, gathering his composure, Norton continued with his questioning of Falcon.

"You said that you saw my client shoot Mr. Frazier," he began.

"Yes."

"Did he, and he alone, shoot Mr. Frazier?"

"No."

"No? What do you mean no? I believe you just stated that you saw him shoot Frazier. Now you say he didn't?"

"The question you asked was did he, and he alone, shoot Frazier," Falcon replied. "The answer is no. All of them were shooting at Mr. Frazier."

"All of them were shooting at Mr. Fra-

307

zier," Norton said. He walked back to his table and picked up a piece of paper. "Mr. Falcon, I have here the coroner's report. According to the coroner, Mr. Frazier suffered four bullet wounds." He looked up from the paper. "I believe you said there were six men in the bank, and all six were shooting?"

"Yes."

"All six were shooting, yet only four bullets hit Mr. Frazier," Norton said. He continued. "That means at least two of the shooters missed, doesn't it? And in fact, isn't it possible that all but one may have missed?"

"It's possible, I suppose," Falcon admitted.

"What is impossible is that all six shooters hit him."

"Obviously, not all six shooters hit him."

"Obviously," Norton repeated. "All right, let us, for the sake of argument, say that four of the shooters hit him. One bullet struck Mr. Frazier in the lung and, according to the coroner, would *probably* have proven to be fatal. Another struck him in the abdomen, which *may* have been fatal. A third struck him in the arm and would not have been fatal. A fourth struck him in the forehead and, according to the coroner, it was *this* shot that killed him."

Norton put the paper down. "Did Mr. Carney fire the shot that hit Mr. Frazier in the head?"

"I don't know," Falcon answered.

"No, of course there is no way you could know that, is there? Did he fire the shot that hit him in the lung?"

"I don't know."

"Did he fire the shot that hit Mr. Frazier in the abdomen?"

"I don't know."

"Did Mr. Carney fire the shot that hit Mr. Frazier in the arm?"

"I don't know," Falcon repeated for the fourth time.

"Indeed, sir, the truth is, you can't even testify as to whether or not the bullet my client fired hit Mr. Frazier at all, can you?"

"No," Falcon said.

"Let me ask you this, Mr. MacCallister. Given the testimony we have just heard, if you were sitting in the jury, could you say, without a shadow of a doubt, that Mr. Carney killed Mr. Frazier?"

"Objection, Your Honor, calls for a conclusion," Nye said.

"Sustained. You do not need to answer that, Mr. MacCallister, and the jury is instructed to draw no inference from the question."

"Your Honor, I have no further questions of this witness," Norton said.

"Redirect?" the judge asked.

"Mr. MacCallister, can you state, from observable fact, that Carney was shooting?"

"Yes, he was shooting," Falcon answered.

"I'm sure the jury knows, and if they do not know, I will remind them during my summation, that in the commission of a felony, all participants are equally guilty," Nye said. He walked over to the exhibit table and picked up the coronor's report. "So you see, it doesn't matter which one of these bullets came from Carney's gun . . . or indeed . . . if any of them came from his gun."

Nye sat down.

"Witness is excused," Judge Blair said.

Falcon took his seat beside Kathleen. "Whew," he said, shaking his head. "I sure hope you do better than I did."

Kathleen mumbled something, but didn't look directly at him.

"Prosecution calls Miss Kathleen Coyle," Nye said.

After being sworn in, Kathlean took her seat. At the beginning, her testimony was very much like Falcon's. She told of going to the bank to make a deposit for the Gold

Strike. She also told of seeing the fire, and seeing Frazier and Mitchum standing by the window, watching the fire.

"And then what happened?" Nye asked.

"Well, like Mr. MacCallister said, six masked men came into the bank."

"Was Mr. Carney one of the six?" Nye asked.

Kathleen nodded. "Yes."

"And you know this because at one point during the robbery he pulled his mask down?"

"Yes."

"Did you see Mr. Frazier get killed?"

"Yes."

"How was he killed?"

Kathleen was quiet for a long moment and Nye, who had looked toward the jury to gauge their reaction to her testimony, turned back toward her when he realized that she had gone a long time without answering the question.

"Miss Coyle?" He said. "Can you tell us what happened?"

"I don't know. It all happened so fast, it was all so confusing with everyone shooting. I mean, I know it was an accident and he was only trying to help, but I think it is entirely possible that Mr. Frazier was killed by a bullet from Mr. MacCallister's gun."

"What?" Falcon shouted, leaping from his seat.

"Order!" Judge Blair shouted, banging his gavel on the desk. "Order!"

TWENTY-TWO

When the jury was dismissed for deliberation, Falcon turned to Kathleen.

"Kathleen, how could you possibly say that one of my bullets might have killed Frazier? I wasn't even shooting. You know my gun was in the spittoon."

"But you were shooting," Kathleen said. "You killed Jerry Snyder that morning, and you wounded Will."

"Yes, but that was afterward," Falcon said. "That took place on the street in front of . . . who's Will?"

"Hey!" someone shouted. "The jury is comin' back."

"What do you mean, comin' back? They just left," another said.

Everyone in the gallery looked toward the side door and saw Ed Wales, the jury foreman, coming back in. They also saw a tall man with dark eyes and a black, sweeping mustache with him. Johnny Purvis was holding a pistol to Wales's head.

"Order in the court!" Johnny shouted. Then he laughed a high-pitched, almost insane giggle. "Order in the court," he repeated. "I've always wanted to do that. Ever'body sit down now!"

"How dare you come into my court!" Judge Blair shouted angrily.

"How dare I? Because I'm holdin' a gun to this man's head, that's how dare I," Johnny said. "Now, when I said for ever'body to sit down, that means you too, Judge. Sit down now, or I'll blow this man's head off!"

"I knew you'd come for me, Johnny!" Carney said.

"We're family, Carney, and family always sticks together. Ain't that right, Girly?" he said to Kathleen.

Kathleen didn't answer.

Johnny pushed Wales in ahead of him. There was another man behind him.

"Poke, give your gun to Carney," Johnny ordered the man behind him.

"What? What do you mean, give my gun to him? What am I goin' to use?"

"Girly, get the sheriff's gun and bring it to Poke," Johnny ordered.

"Keep her out of it, Purvis," Falcon said. "She doesn't have anything to do with this."

"It's all right, Falcon, I'll do it," Kathleen said. "There have been enough people killed already. I don't want anyone else to get hurt."

Kathleen got up from her seat in the gallery and walked over to Sheriff Gibson to relieve him of his gun.

"Be careful with that, Miss Coyle," Sheriff Gibson said as she took the gun from him.

"I will be," Kathleen said in a quiet, hesitant voice.

Holding the pistol by her thumb and forefinger, Kathleen took it over to Johnny, then held it out toward him. The gallery looked on in fear and nervousness.

Johnny shook his head. "No, don't give it to me. You take the gun, Poke."

Poke walked over to Kathleen. "Give me that!" he growled at her, jerking the gun away from her.

Falcon pointed to Johnny. "I'm warning you, Purvis," he shouted angrily. "Don't you hurt that girl!"

Johnny smiled, then put his arm around her and pulled her to him. He kissed her on the cheek, and to Falcon's shocked surprise, Kathleen kissed him back. The rest of the gallery gasped in surprise as well.

"Now, tell me, MacCallister," Johnny said to Falcon. "Just why would me 'n Carney want to hurt our sister?"

"Your sister?" Falcon asked in a shocked voice.

Johnny nodded. "Yep. Girly is our sister. Her real name is Kathleen, but me an' Carney has always called her Girly. Right, Girly?"

Kathleen said nothing, but she continued to look at Falcon with what looked like an expression of shame and contrition.

"Oh, and that business up in Miles City where I broke into her room? We set that up just so's she could get close to you. And the whole reason she took a job here in the saloon was so's she could help set everything up for us to rob the bank. Only thing is, we didn't know nothin' about there not bein' no money there yet." Johnny laughed out loud. "The money didn't get there till today."

"You son of a bitch!" Sheriff Gibson shouted out loud. "Are you saying you robbed the bank today?"

"Yep, while you folks was all busy with the trial, we was busy robbin' the bank. Pretty smart, huh? One hunnert and eleven thousand dollars we got," Johnny said. "Not as much as I thought, but you got to admit, that's not bad. Come on, Carney and Girly. Poke, you keep this fella covered till we get

316

out of here."

"Don't worry, I got 'im," Poke said.

Poke stepped up behind the frightened Wales and pointed his pistol at his head.

Johnny Purvis, Carney, Kathleen, and Poke started to leave. As they passed by Falcon, Sheriff Gibson, who was on the opposite side of the room, suddenly threw a chair through the window.

Distracted by it, Poke looked toward the sound. As he did so, Falcon pushed the jury foreman out of the way, then jumped Poke and grabbed his gun. They struggled for the gun and it went off.

"Oh!" Kathleen shouted. "Johnny, I've been shot!" She fell.

Carney looked back toward her and stopped.

"Come on, Carney, let's get out of here!"

"Girly's been shot," Carney said.

"Let's get out of here!" Johnny repeated. Johnny shot back into the courtroom, and everyone screamed and yelled and fell to the floor.

"I'll kill the first man that sticks his head out the door!" he shouted.

During this time the struggle between Falcon and Poke continued; then there was a second shot, muffled because it was at point-blank range.

Falcon backed away, now with the gun in his hand. As Poke went down, clutching the wound in his stomach, Falcon ran to the front door.

Johnny, Carney, and the three who had waited out front were gone, leaving Kathleen and Poke behind them.

"Damn!" Falcon said angrily.

Falcon went back into the courthouse. The doctor, who had come to see the trial, was kneeling beside Kathleen.

"How bad is she?" Falcon asked.

The doctor looked up at Falcon, and though he said nothing, he made a small, barely perceptible shake of his head.

"Falcon," Kathleen said in a weak voice.

Falcon knelt beside her.

"I'm sorry," she said. "They were my brothers. We had different fathers, but the same mother. Johnny Purvis and Will Carney raised me. I . . . I had to do it."

Falcon didn't say anything.

"All the killing," she said. "Poor Mr. Keith and Mr. Garrison, Mr. Mitchum, and Gordon. I . . . I had no idea they would be doing anything like that. I'm so sorry . . . I didn't know."

"Was anyone hurt when Purvis shot into the courthouse?" Falcon asked.

"No," the doctor said. "The only other

one is the man you struggled with, and he's dead."

"Falcon, do you . . . do you really think I could have made it on the stage in New York?" Kathleen asked, her voice growing weaker.

"I'm sure you could have," Falcon said.

"That would have really been something," she said. "Johnny and Will laughed at me for it. But that would have really been some . . ." she breathed her last.

"Go after them, Falcon," Kohrs said. "Don't worry about the cattle. For you, I will get some prime stock, and at a good price."

Falcon nodded. He knew and trusted Kohrs, and if Kohrs said he would get prime stock at a good price, Falcon could take that to the bank.

"Thanks," Falcon said.

"Falcon?" Sheriff Gibson said.

Falcon looked up and saw that the sheriff was holding his guns out to him.

Falcon gave the sheriff's pistol back to him; then he took his own Colt and slipped it into his holster. After that, he took the derringer and pushed it down into the top of his boot.

"I know you aren't much for badges," Gibson said. "But in front of these witnesses, I'm deputizing you. It'll keep you legal, at least as long as you are in Albany County."

"I'm not going to stop at the county line," Falcon said.

Gibson nodded. "Nor would I expect you to."

"I'll just be getting my things; then I'm going after them."

Back in his room at the boardinghouse, Falcon changed from the black suit and white shirt he had worn during the court case into trail clothes of jeans, long-sleeved shirt, and vest. He put his hat on, and was just tying up his bedroll when he heard the door open behind him.

Because no one had knocked, Falcon whirled toward the opening door, pulling and cocking his gun in the same motion. Raising his pistol into the firing position, he saw Frances Martin standing in the door.

To Falcon's surprise, Frances did not react in fear to his sudden draw against her. In fact, she stood in the doorway as calmly as if she were carrying on a casual conversation with him. She was also wearing clothes that were nearly identical to what he was wearing: pants, a long-sleeve shirt, a vest, and a low-crowned black hat. She wasn't

320

wearing a pistol, but she was carrying two rifles.

"Oh, it's you," Falcon said. "What are you doing dressed like that?"

"You're going after Johnny and the others, aren't you?"

"I am."

"So am I."

"The hell you are."

"I'm going after the men who killed my son," Frances said.

Falcon shook his head. "Frances, look, I know you are a good shot," he said. "In fact, you are one of the best shots I've ever seen, man or woman. But you aren't going with me."

"Why not? Don't you think I have a right to go after the ones who killed my boy?"

"I don't deny that," Falcon said.

"Then give me one good reason I can't go with you. You've already acknowledged that I'm a good shot."

Falcon sighed. "Yes, you're a good shot, all right. But we won't be shooting at targets on hay bales. We'll be shooting at men. I don't need anyone with me who might get squeamish about killing someone."

"Even if they need killing?"

"You don't understand," Falcon said. "When you are in a situation like this, it doesn't matter whether they need killing or not. You don't have time to analyze the situation. If you have to kill, you kill."

"Like in a war?" Frances asked. "In war people kill people, simply because they are on the other side. They don't stop to think whether or not they need killing, or whether they are good men, or whether they have families. They just kill them because it is their job to kill them."

"Yes, you might say it is something like that," Falcon agreed.

"I understand that."

"Understanding it and being able to do it are two different things."

"I can do it," Frances said.

"Frances, look, I know you want revenge for Gordon, and I don't blame you, but . . ."

"Falcon, when you were at the funeral, did you hear the preacher say Gordon's whole name?"

"What?" Falcon asked, wondering what the question had to do with this.

"Did you hear the preacher give Gordon's whole name?"

"Yes, Gordon Martin," Falcon replied.

"It was Gordon O'Neil Martin," Frances corrected.

Falcon still didn't know where Frances was going with this.

"My maiden name was O'Neil," Frances said. "And my mother's maiden name was Fitzpatrick. "My whole name was Frances Fitzpatrick O'Neil."

The name still didn't quite register with Falcon.

"You do remember the Phantom of Devil's Den that Mr. Caulder was talking about, don't you?" Frances asked. "The sharpshooter who killed twenty-three Rebel soldiers? Actually, it was only nine. These things always do have a way of getting exaggerated."

"Nine," Falcon said. "And you know it was nine because?"

"Because it was me," Frances said. "I was the Phantom of Devil's Den."

"What?" Falcon asked. "Look here, Frances, are you trying to tell me that you were a sharpshooter during the war?"

"Yes."

Falcon shook his head. "Impossible," he said.

"Why impossible?" Frances asked. "If you read your history, you'll see that there were a lot of women who disguised themselves as men to fight in the war. Even in our Revolutionary War there was Molly Pitcher. I'm not the only woman ever to do this."

"But why in heaven's name would your

father let you do such a thing?"

"My father had no choice in the matter," Frances said. "He was killed at Chancellorsville. My mother died of a broken heart soon after. I had no one left in my family and I wanted revenge. So you can see, this isn't new to me."

Falcon looked deep into the woman's eyes and realized she wasn't lying to him.

"Do you have a horse?" he asked.

"Yes, I have a horse. It was Gordon's horse, but it is a good one."

"All right," Falcon said, nodding. "I'll let you come."

Smiling, Frances shook her head. "You still don't understand, do you, Falcon?"

"Understand what?"

"There is no 'letting me come' to it. I was going on this hunt, with or without you."

Falcon smiled. "Damn, woman," he said. "You may just be wildcat enough to come in useful after all."

TWENTY-THREE

Riding hard, Johnny, Carney, Eddie, Gabe, and Pete reached Last Chance just before nightfall. Putting on their red scarves, they galloped through the draw and into the hidden valley itself.

There were about fifteen people in Last Chance, counting the men and women, and they all gathered to see what had caused the riders to come in at a gallop. The horses were breathing hard, and they were covered with a foam of sweat.

"Johnny, what is it? What's goin' on?" Quincy asked.

"Hello, Quincy," Johnny said. "I'm glad you're here. I'm going to need every man."

"You're going to need every man for what?"

"We snatched Carney out of jail," Johnny said. "There will be a posse comin' out here for sure. We're goin' to have to fight 'em off."

Quincy shook his head no. "Huh-uh," he said. "You ain't goin' to get me in on this. I didn't take part in whatever you've been doin', and I ain't fightin' no posse for you."

"Fifty dollars to anyone who stays and helps us fight 'em off!" Johnny shouted.

"Fifty dollars? I wouldn't stay for five hundred dollars," Quincy said. He looked at the others who were living at Last Chance. "You folks can stay and get killed if you want, but I'm getting out of here."

"Me too."

"So am I."

Within minutes everyone except the ones who had ridden with Johnny were saddled, men and women alike. Quincy rode over to where Johnny and the others of his group were rubbing down their horses.

"I wish you good luck, Johnny," Quincy said. "But you got to admit that you got your ownself into this mess. You got no right to think any of us should stick around to get ourselves killed tryin' to help you."

"I understand," Johnny said.

"If you get through this, maybe we'll get together again sometime."

"Maybe," Johnny said.

"Come on, folks," Quincy called to the others. "Let's get out of here before the posse gets here."

Johnny watched them until the last person had disappeared through the draw; then he turned to the others with a big smile.

"All right, boys," he said. "No need for us to share the money with anyone now. It's all ours."

"Johnny," Pete said nervously. "You really think they will send a posse after us?"

Johnny shook his head. "They can't. Sheriff Gibson is in Albany County. We're in Carbon County. He ain't got no jurisdiction here."

Pete smiled. "Then there ain't nobody goin' to be comin, is there? You just got rid of the others so's they wouldn't know about the money."

"MacCallister will be comin'," Carney said.

"What?" Pete asked.

"MacCallister will be comin' after us," Carney repeated.

"How is he even goin' to know where we are?" Pete asked.

"He'll know," Johnny said. "That son of a bitch can track a bird through the air. We may as well get ready for him."

"Why do we have to get ready for him?" Eddie asked. "Why don't we just divide up the money now and all of us go our own way?"

"You want to be dogged by MacCallister for the rest of your life?" Johnny asked. "If we don't kill him now, he'll track ever'one us down."

"I agree," Gabe said. "I've heard about MacCallister, and I know he's just the kind of son of a bitch who would be after us for the rest of our lives. It's best to take care of him now, while we are all together. What do you have in mind, Johnny?"

"Gabe, I want you and Pete to be posted on either side of the draw that leads into here," Johnny said. "And Eddie, I want you on top of the big rock at the end of the pass."

"Hell, what do we need all that for, Johnny? We only need one man watchin' the pass," Eddie said.

"Just do what I said," Johnny ordered without elaboration.

"What about you and Carney?" Pete asked. "Where you going to be?"

"I'm going to put Carney in the loft of the barn," Johnny replied. "I'll be on the second floor of the house. If Falcon makes it by you three, we'll have a good shot at him soon as he comes into the valley. And by that time, you three will be behind him. We'll have him in a cross fire."

Eddie laughed. "You act like we was about

to get attacked by an army or somethin', what with postin' lookouts ever'where. You sure you don't have a couple of them Gatling guns hid out some'ers?"

"I wish I did have a couple of Gatling guns," Johnny said.

"Are you afraid of MacCallister, Johnny?" Eddie asked.

"You damn right I'm afraid of him. You will be too, if you have any sense. Now, you folks get posted like I told you to."

"All right, all right," Eddie said. "We'll get where you told us to get. Hell, I might even see if I can round up a Gatling gun or two," he added with a sardonic chuckle.

"Just do what I said," Johnny growled.

Johnny and Carney watched the three men leave to get into position.

"You want me to get in the barn now?" Carney asked.

"Yeah" Johnny said. He pointed to the second-story window of the house. "I'll be up there."

"All right," Carney said.

"Johnny?"

"Yeah?"

"We shouldn't of left Girly like that."

"She's likely dead by now and we couldn't of helped her if we stayed," Johnny said. "Besides, look at it this way. That's just one more reason for us to kill MacCallister."

It had not been hard to track them. There were five men, riding hard and making no effort to hide their trail. It was late afternoon when Falcon and Frances reached the opening of the pass, and now they were crouched down behind a rock outcropping about two hundred yards from the opening of the draw.

Taking off his hat, Falcon climbed to just below the top of the rocks and looked through the binoculars he had bought to follow Gordon's footrace. Holding the binoculars made him think of young Gordon lying dead, shot down in the street by the men he was chasing.

The sun was low in the west, and though the day wasn't unbearably hot, the sun was bright enough to be oppressive to someone who was trying to keep a sharp watch. The gnats were out also, and when one of the lookouts slapped at one of them, Falcon caught just a glimpse of the movement.

"Do you see anyone?" Frances asked in a quiet voice.

"Yes," Falcon said. "He's up on top, on the left, about twenty-five yards back from the lip, just where that side of the draw flattens." Falcon handed his binoculars to Frances, but she waved them off.

"I can do better with this," she said. Since they'd arrived, she'd fitted a scope onto her rifle, and now she looked through the scope. "There he is," she said.

"Is that the rifle you used in the war?"

"Yes," Frances said. She smiled. "I know what you are thinking. This is a Whitworth and was used primarily by the South. But it was the most accurate rifle in the war and I came by one very early."

"No, what I was thinking is that it is a single-shot," Falcon said. "That might be a problem."

"One shot is all I've ever needed before," Frances said.

"You think you can hit him from here?" Falcon asked, talking about the man they had spotted.

"Yes. Do you want me to?" Frances pulled the hammer back and raised the rifle.

"Yes, but not yet," Falcon said, stopping her. "Wait until you get my signal."

"What kind of signal?"

Falcon pointed toward the mouth of the draw. "I'm going to try and work my way all the way down to this end of the pass without being seen," he said. "When I get there, I'll wave at you. That's when I want you to take out the lookout. You are far enough away here that by the time the sound of the shot reaches the others, I'll be inside."

"All right," Frances said.

There was no way anyone on horseback could approach the narrow opening of the draw without being seen, but ever since they had arrived, Falcon had been looking for an alternate route, and now he believed he had found one. Leaving his position of concealment behind the rock, Falcon started working his way along the bottom of a steep cliff. There were several places where he was able to go down into long, narrow cuts that allowed him to advance without being seen.

The advantage of this route was that it eventually put him in position at the very opening of the draw. The disadvantage was that, while he couldn't be seen, neither could he see the lookout. That was why he was going to have to depend upon Frances.

It had taken him about ten minutes to work his way there. Now, looking back to where he knew Frances was, he saw what a good place they had discovered. He knew exactly where to look, but he couldn't see her. He could only hope that she could see him. He waved at her, then waited.

The question as to whether or not she could see him was answered within seconds, because he saw the muzzle flash of her Whitworth.

With his pistol in hand, he rushed into the pass. The lookout was falling even as the sound of the gunshot reached him; a heavy boom that rolled down the draw, gathering resonance from the walls and erupting at the far end in a thunderous roar.

"Pete!" a voice shouted from the top of the draw on the opposite side.

Damn! Falcon hadn't seen a second man. Looking up now, he saw, and was seen at the same time.

The two men fired at each other, the pistol shots sounding simultaneously. Like the rifle shot before, the noise of the two shots echoed back and forth until it was impossible to tell how many shots had been fired.

The man on top who was shooting at Falcon missed, but Falcon did not miss, and his target tumbled down, falling within a few feet of the other one. Both men were now lying dead, belly-down on the rocky floor of the pass.

Falcon stood there for a moment, looking down at the two men. Then he heard the loud boom of the Whitworth again, followed by a grunt of pain. Looking up, he saw a third man tumbling down.

"He had a bead on you," Frances said, coming up behind him.

"Get your rifle reloaded and come with

me," Falcon said.

"I brought this one too," Frances said, holding up a Winchester. She laid the Whitworth down. "We can always pick this one up when we're finished."

Falcon and Frances moved through the draw until they reached the open area of the little valley.

"Look at this," Frances said in awe. "Who would have ever thought there would be such a . . ." Frances let out a gasp, and Falcon saw a mist of blood fly up from the impact of the bullet. Frances went down.

"Frances!" Falcon shouted. "No!"

A second bullet whizzed by, kicking up the dirt around him.

Looking up, Falcon saw a little puff of gun smoke drifting away from the open window of the barn loft. He ran toward the barn, dodging two more bullets, one from the barn, and one, he noticed, from the top floor of the nearby house.

Dashing through the open door of the barn, Falcon dived into a pile of straw. He rolled over, then looked up at the floor of the loft. The loft floor was made of weathered planking with fairly wide gaps between the planks.

Falcon lay very quiet and very still.

"Johnny! Johnny, can you see him?"

From the voice, Falcon knew that Carney was in the loft above him.

"He went into the barn!" a muffled voice replied.

"Where?"

"How the hell am I supposed to know? You are the one in the barn. Look for him!"

As Falcon continued to look up at the loft, he saw movement between the cracks. He couldn't see Carney, but he was able to figure out where he was, just by the difference of light and shadow. He fired three quick shots, heard Carney groan, then heard him fall.

Moving quickly, Falcon ran to the ladder, then climbed up to the loft. Peering just over the edge of the loft, he saw Carney lying there in a pool of spreading blood. Some of the blood was already beginning to drip down between the cracks.

Cautiously, Falcon stepped up onto the loft, then walked over and looked down at Carney.

Carney was dead.

"Carney! Carney, did you get him?" Johnny called.

Falcon was quiet.

"Did you get him, Carney?"

Falcon made his voice sound strained. "I killed him, Johnny, but I'm hit."

"How bad are you hit?"

Falcon smiled. Johnny bought it.

"How bad are you hit?" he asked again.

Falcon decided not to push his luck a second time.

"I'm comin' over," Johnny called back.

Falcon moved back into the shadows of the loft so he couldn't be seen right away. Quickly, he reloaded, then he waited.

He heard the door to the house close. A moment later, he heard Johnny come in through the open door of the barn.

"Carney? Carney, are you up there?" he called. "Listen, Carney, I was thinkin'. Maybe I'd better take all the money with me, you know, to put it in a safe place? Then, after you're feelin' better, you can have your share. Carney?"

Falcon still didn't answer.

"Carney, I'm comin' up."

As Falcon waited, he could hear Johnny coming up the ladder, one step at a time.

"Carney, what the hell?" Johnny said when he reached the top rung. He stepped onto the loft floor, then came over to look down at the body of his brother.

"Hello, Johnny," Falcon said, stepping out of the shadows.

"MacCallister!" Johnny said. "Carney told me you were dead!"

"No, he didn't," Falcon said. "I told you. And I lied."

Johnny raised his pistol and thumbed back the hammer, but before he could pull the trigger, a finger of flame spit from the barrel of Falcon's .44. A black hole appeared between Johnny's eyes. The bullet didn't go all the way through, but the impact caused the hydrostatic action of the blood and brain fluid to blow a half-dollar-size chunk of bone, brain tissue, and blood out the back of his head.

In honor of Frances Martin, the cattle auction was postponed for one day in order to conduct her funeral. It was large and well attended by all, including the assembled cattle barons.

The auction itself was large, and because all the money that was taken from the bank was returned, it was a happy and successful event. The only hitch came when, at the last moment, Falcon decided he wasn't going to buy any Herefords at all.

"Why not?" Kohrs asked when he saw that Falcon wasn't going to bid.

"I don't know," Falcon said. "Somehow there seems to be a sense of permanence in buying Herefords, as if I am ready to settle down. I'm just not."

Kohrs smiled. "I understand," he said. "Even I sometimes get the desire to go back to sea. I know exactly what you mean."

Before he left Laramie, Falcon paid one last visit to the cemetery, visiting, briefly, the graves of Mitchum, Gordon, and Frances. He hadn't planned to visit Kathleen's grave, but he did, and he wound up spending more time there than he did at any of the other graves.

"I don't guess I can blame you all that much," he had said quietly. "You didn't choose your family."

There were no flowers on Kathleen's grave, but there were several on Mitchum's grave, and it was very close by, so Falcon picked up a couple of roses and dropped them onto the mound of dirt.

"I don't think they'll be bothering you anymore now. I've got a feeling that you and your brothers went to different places."

As the train hurtled through the approaching darkness, Falcon, who was riding in a parlor car, tilted his seat back to get comfortable. He would be in MacCallister Valley by noon tomorrow. How long he stayed there was anyone's guess.

ABOUT THE AUTHOR

William W. Johnstone is the *USA Today* bestselling author of over 130 books, including the popular *Ashes, Mountain Man,* and *Last Gunfighter* series.